Blood
and
Black Roses

A Dark Bouquet of Vampires,
Romance and Horror

Sophia diGregorio

2012
Winter Tempest Books

Copyright © 2012 Sophia diGregorio

All rights reserved.

ISBN-10: 061573992X
ISBN-13: 978-0615739922
Winter Tempest Books

DEDICATION

In memory of my grandparents.

CONTENTS

Introduction	1
Blood and Money: The Vampire and the Robber	5
Blood on the Stage: The Vampire and the Stalking Victim	17
Blood and Linen: The Vampire and the Runaway Wife	51
Blood and Black Lace: The Vampire and the Call Girl	77
Blood and Stilettos: The Diary of a Vampire Stripper	103
Blood and Cashmere: The Vampire and the Rich Girl	167

INTRODUCTION

Only in recent years has the vampire in literary horror become a thing of beauty and the object of romantic longing. The depiction of the vampire as a romantic anti-hero is a new element in the canon of this genre of fiction. In fact, the difference between the vampires of the 19th century and those of the present is so great that the two barely seem like the same being.

In previous incarnations, the vampire was a remorseless, blood-sucking wraith, damned to live only by night and cursed with an uncontrollable thirst for the blood of the innocent. He was a hideous supernatural being, loathed and feared by his victims who was created by being bitten and drained of blood by another vampire. A human being could, also, be transformed into a vampire by his own evil deeds or psychological make-up. Because he was pure evil, he could be repelled by the crucifix, a wreath of garlic and sometimes by sunlight.

By contrast, the new vampire is not so much evil as

he is morally complex, therefore, he is not always relegated to the darkness, but can sometimes live in the light and is not necessarily responsive to Christian symbols or superstitions. He is not ugly or loathsome, although his beauty may be imperfect. He may commit unwholesome acts according to his nature, but he is redeemable because has a conscience and a sense of remorse for his deeds. He has more control over his violent urges than his predecessors and may even be a humanist who chooses to feed only on the blood of evil men or animals.

Theories abound as to why vampires are the new popular romantic heroes and we shall add one more here:

The vampire is the new knight in shining armor for a deeply troubled era. The old romantic hero was valiant, true and pure of heart like Prince Phillip who rescues the princess in Sleeping Beauty or Sir Gawain from whom purity of heart is required to fulfill his destiny.

The new hero is flawed in proportion to our presently flawed world, where everything is turned upside down and the very institutions and people we trust most frequently turn out to be the most diabolically evil villains. The vampire is the new, romantic ideal in a world so corrupt that it is impossible to envision moral perfection, even in a hero.

Byronic anti-heroes have always been beloved by readers of Gothic horror and romance because their complexity makes them more interesting. But, the vampire as an anti-hero isn't just slightly flawed like Heathcliff or Mr. Rochester, he is very flawed, in fact, he is literally a monster.

About the stories in this collection:

The protagonists in these stories are all strong women. The real villains are their most trusted fathers, husbands, boyfriends and the police. This is a reflection of real life for many people, wherein benevolent-seeming people and institutions psychopathically betray us by concealing their true natures.

By contrast, the vampire does not hide his true identity or his motives. Because the vampire offers free will and immortality, he is a means of escape, redemption and the establishment of a new, more livable life. Unlike the real villains in the story, the vampire never tries to take anything from the protagonist.

While the vampires may be killers, they apply reason and moral conscience to their actions, whereas the real villains are sociopaths without remorse, redemption or morals.

Integral to the theme of some of these stories are descriptions of violence, including domestic abuse in Blood and Linen, which the reader should be prepared for, although, they are only explicit enough to convey what is necessary to understand the characters' motivation. While these stories are entirely fictional, they depict some realistic aspects of adult life and are not intended for minors. The author sincerely hopes you will enjoy these tales of romantic vampires and horror.

Sophia diGregorio

BLOOD AND MONEY:
THE VAMPIRE AND THE ROBBER

Blue Harbor City Police Department

<u>Voluntary Statement</u>

Date: December 3, 2010

Name: Deborah Drucker

Waiver of Rights

Do you understand your rights? <u>Yes</u>

Are you willing to waive your rights and make a confession? <u>Yes</u>

Catherine Adams is my neighbor and dearest friend. We bought our homes, which are side-by-side in the same neighborhood, in the same year only a month apart.

At that time, my husband was serving in the Middle East as a Marine captain and Catherine was married, too. Since neither of us really knew anyone else in the neighborhood or had any children, we began our own tradition of daily lunches and coffee. That's how we got to be friends.

Our lives seemed to parallel each other in a number of ways. Each of us had ambitions that were unrealized due to circumstances beyond our control.

I wanted to finish law school, but I was unable to because I ran out of funds and was unwilling to go any further into debt on student loans. The way tuition was rising, it was no longer a financially viable option. Catherine was once a successful real estate broker, but she lost her company and all of her savings and investments about the time of the banking bailouts.

In spite of these setbacks, things were still going reasonably well for us. We often congratulated ourselves for making such good choices, despite the sea of adversity that surrounded us.

One day, I looked at Catherine over our usual lunchtime coffee and sandwiches and for the first time, I noticed deep lines of worry forming on her brow. She looked tired, in fact, she looked downright haggard.

I didn't want to pry but it seemed to me that something was wrong. I had noticed over the past days that she looked uncharacteristically unkempt and the cheerfulness seemed to be slowly draining out of her.

So, I asked her if everything was all right.

"I don't know," she said. "But, something seems different about Justin lately. He has been very cruel and he's becoming more and more violent. I've never seen him like this before."

Justin was her husband of nearly twelve years and, at that moment, she didn't understand entirely what was happening. He had recently lost a good job and, faced with no decent employment prospects, he was slowly succumbing to alcohol and mental illness.

Weeks later, I recall seeing the crazed look in his eyes as he was packing his personal belongings and leaving the house. That was the last time I saw him and a few weeks afterward, he died in a drunken automobile accident. The only consolation she received was that she didn't have to put up with his abuses, anymore.

About that same time, although the exact dates are a little fuzzy to me because it was a time of such turmoil for us, I received correspondence from the U.S. Marine Corps telling me that my husband would not be coming home. Afterward, I found myself overwhelmed by a confusion of bureaucratic red tape, so that I doubted I would ever receive any compensation for his death.

Again, Catherine's life and mine had formed a parallel to each other. We were both freshly widowed, in a state of shock and jobless with no prospects. What's more, we were deeply in debt in houses we could no longer afford and had no hope of selling for even one-third of their original value. We didn't know what to do.

We were in a state of deep despair, but the more we talked about what had happened to us, the more angry we became. We determined over coffee that we'd been robbed by the banks, that they were the root cause of the circumstances we found ourselves in.

As we began to discuss how we had been deprived, this fomented in us a rage born of self-righteous indignation, which gave us courage. We literally had nothing left to lose. We decided we would just take back what we were owed - no more and no less.

We calculated the monetary value of all of our lost equity, lost education, lost opportunities and increases in taxation. Allowing for inflation, we arrived at a figure right down to the last penny, which had been stolen from us.

Then, we chose a major bank, one of the corporate welfare recipients responsible for our present troubles, and began to formulate a plan for robbing it. We would be in disguise, but we thought it would be prudent to choose a branch location some distance away from our own homes to stage the robbery.

Robbery! When I think of it, even now, I cannot believe we actually followed through with such a plan, however, we were both convinced that this was our only chance to recoup what we had lost. And, given the dire situation we were faced with, succeeding at it was our last hope!

We knew we needed a getaway car that would not be easy to trace. After researching the best method for stealing a car without risking damage to it, we devised a scheme to obtain keys for the two main cars we planned to use and the contingency vehicles.

We tried to back up every aspect of our plan in some way and rehearsed exactly how we would do it.

Since I'm the taller of the two of us and appeared more transformed by the disguise, we decided that I would actually commit the robbery and Catherine would drive the getaway car.

On the designated date, we waited until near closing time of the chosen bank before I went in disguised as a delivery boy. I carried a gun, but no ammunition. We didn't want to hurt anyone; we only wanted what is rightfully ours.

Things went off without a hitch. It was so much easier than I ever imagined to just walk into a bank and leave with the money.

Just as we planned, we drove the first getaway car to the point of exchange where we took a second stolen car and ditched our disguises.

By this time, it was getting dark. We had our route

home mapped out. It doesn't seem possible to me, even now, that we could have made a wrong turn, but apparently, we did.

Instead of going in the direction of home we were traveling in some unknown direction to some unknown place.

Huge drops of rain began forming on the windshield and soon afterward it became torrents. The sheets of falling rain which obscured our vision only further confounded us and the thunder and lightning served to heighten our anxiety, however, we did not lose hope that we would find our way home.

Then, Catherine noticed that a warning light flashed on the dashboard in some unfamiliar symbol. We didn't know what it meant, but right after that happened we found ourselves sitting at the side of the road on a remote highway. The car wouldn't start, again! We didn't know what else to do, so Catherine tucked our money safely into her underclothes, then we quickly abandoned the car and started walking in hopes of finding shelter.

We must have walked a couple of miles before we spotted a dim light emanating from a house sitting some distance off the road. It was the first structure of any kind we had seen.

In desperation, we walked past the black iron gate and up the winding driveway, shrouded by huge knotted and twisted trees with low-hanging branches. In between the flashes of lightning, we could see that the pathway we we walked upon and the stairs we climbed to get to the front door were old and crumbling, as if no one had paid attention to them for a very long time.

But, we pinned our hopes on the dim light still softly emanating from inside an upper story room of this isolated, crumbling edifice, which had seen its glory days in a past century. It was decrepit, but nonetheless formidable.

I cannot be sure whether it was because of the icy, cold rain or some intuitive sense of foreboding, but a cold shudder ran through me as we raised the huge knocker on the front door and allowed it to drop down, sending a resounding echo through the gnarled trees and the decaying front porch.

Some time passed and there was no response. My imagination began to run wild with unpleasant possibilities. This might be the family home of some ancient matriarch with gray hair and a grandmotherly smile or it might just as easily be the lair of a serial killer who preyed on stranded motorists.

In those moments, my anxiety mounted to such an extent that I was mostly relieved when no answer came. We turned around and resolved to keep on walking until we found some kind of shelter.

Behind us we heard the loud creak of the front door opening. We both turned to see who was there.

At the door, stood a little, misshapen man with a small, croaking voice that corresponded to his diminutive stature. "Who's there?" he called.

Catherine spoke. "Our car broke down. We just need some place to get dry until this storm passes."

"Come in!" said the little man. And we gratefully went up the steps and inside.

If the house had electricity, it must have been out because of the raging storm, which was showing no signs of letting up.

We stood, dripping wet, in the main room of the house. A fire was burning in the fireplace in the corner.

Instinctively, we walked toward it. As we stood warming ourselves, we became aware of another presence in the room.

A regal figure sat in a high-backed chair, observing the fire and us.

"Good evening," said the deep, masculine voice from

behind us.

"Good evening, "we answered. Apologetically, we repeated that our car had broken down.

"I am happy to provide you with whatever you need," he said. "My valet is at your service, as am I."

We were soaked to the bone and our shoes were filled with water. "I don't suppose you have any dry clothes we could borrow?" I asked.

"There are rooms full of clothes upstairs. I am sure you will find something to fit you. My valet will show you."

"I just wish we could go home," I whispered to Catherine.

"When it's daylight and the rain stops," she reassured me. "There's no point in trying to figure it out until then."

We were both aware of the importance of saying nothing about our caper or even hinting at it. Nothing more was said as we were both aware that the other could easily let something slip if we said anything, at all.

The little hunchback valet limpingly guided us up the stairs, illuminating our way with a glimmering candelabra held high in one hand.

We were shown into a beautiful room that looked as if it hadn't been touched in decades. There were clothes in the closet, which were dusty and dated, but dry and we were happy to change into them. We were, also, glad to find blankets at our disposal.

After a while, the valet returned to tell us that one of us would be welcome to stay the night in this room and there was another room available for the other one.

I chose to stay while Catherine went down the hall with the valet to a room of her own.

Catherine said, "Good night," to me and I replied, "Goodnight." Little did I know that those would be the last words we would speak to each other.

My anxiety was very great and the constant replaying in my mind of the events of the day rendered me unable to sleep. I didn't know where the little hunchback had taken Catherine, but I decided I would try to find her.

Finding a candle and a box of matches by the nightstand, I went out into the empty hallway. I took care to make as little noise as possible as I walked along the creaking floors.

I began to notice that some doors were slightly ajar and others were completely closed. I reasoned that Catherine would be in a room with a closed door, but so would our host, his valet and anyone else who might be in the house that I didn't know about.

I listened at one of the nearby closed doors, but I heard nothing and upon peering through the keyhole I saw only complete blackness. I repeated this procedure at several closed doors until I reached one from which I heard low voices emanating, a man's and a woman's.

I couldn't make out what they were saying, but when I looked through the keyhole, I saw that the room was illuminated by numerous candles.

I surmised that there were, in fact, other people in the house with us and I lingered for a few moments to ascertain what kind of people they might be. After all, with the recent crime wave, one cannot be too cautious.

Although I had only seen him briefly, I recognized the man of the couple as our host and my initial impression was that I was eavesdropping on a romantic interlude. But, I could not see the woman very well as her head was shrouded in darkness, but her body was exposed.

As I watched them, I became increasingly amused by what I saw and the forbidden thrill of creeping outside the door, undetected, like a voyeur.

The lady was beautiful with the shadows of the room playing on her curvaceous body to her advantage. It struck me, as I watched him working his magic upon her, that he, too, was a handsome man of indiscernible age. His hair was black as coal and contrasted sharply against the ivory pallor of his skin. His features were sharp, almost severe and his eyes, beneath their arched eyebrows, possessed an eerie gleam. I considered, as I scrutinized his features, that he belonged to some bygone era.

The woman was clad in a white, flowing robe, which was completely open in front. He was admiring her nearly nude form, uttering exclamations of pleasure as he ran his hands over her body and kissed her hungrily.

I experienced a vicarious thrill as I peered at the two of them through the keyhole. I felt that it was wrong and I chided myself inwardly, yet I could not seem to pry my eyes away from the keyhole.

He spoke some words to her that I could not discern as he kissed her neck and lips, thrusting his tongue deeply into her mouth without restraint while caressing her hair in a loving fashion.

He lowered his head and I could tell he was engaged in the act of love making, although I could not quite discern what he was doing while she kissed his hair and ran her fingers through it. When he tired of this, he rose and moved his lips to hers, again, and they kissed with a passion such as I have never seen before.

In the next instance, there ensued a tumultuous episode of writhing about on the bed in ecstasy, which went on for some time before it culminated in gasps of delight. Of course, I knew it was wrong for me to invade their privacy in this way, but I was beside myself with excitement at this spectacle of his strong arms holding her, his dark hair brushing against her skin as they cried out unified in their passion. It all seemed so unreal.

I watched as he paused and, again, leaned forward to shower her lips and her neck with kisses only to begin making love to her, again. I could almost feel the heat of their passion radiating through the heavy wooden door.

This went on for some time before, with cries of delight, they swooned and lay rapturously in each other's arms, yet again. They languished in this fashion, speaking words to each other I could not clearly hear, until our host rose and sat upon his knees, then grasping the lady by the hair and revealing her face in the light, he drew her nearer to him. She was willing, longingly caressing his bare chest with her long, slender fingers. He turned her head to one side, so she was facing the door for the first time.

This is when I suddenly recognized the lady as Catherine!

In the next horrifying moment, he sank his teeth into her neck and she writhed in either agony or ecstasy, I could not tell which, as he sucked the blood from her veins like a wild animal feeding on its helpless quarry.

Upon seeing this, I could not suppress a loud gasp of alarm. This startled the two of them and they both stood up very abruptly, as if they suddenly perceived they were being observed.

Only seconds later, I was aware of a tumult coming from downstairs. I heard men shouting and the thunder of feet on the stairs. I was distracted by this, so I did not actually see what happened in the room in the moments that followed.

But, the last thing I remember hearing before the rush of policemen, was the creaking sound of the window sash being thrown up and the clatter of the shutters, followed by the shrill, plaintive cry of bats as they receded into the distance.

I was terrified to see the police clamoring down the hallway at me. Moments later, the police fastened their hands on me and I was read my rights.

As God is my witness! I swear that I do not know where Catherine, our host or the little hunchback valet went. Nor, can I rationally account for what I saw or heard in that room any more than I know what ultimately happened to her or her part of the money. But, it is gone and so is Catherine.

Sophia diGregorio

BLOOD ON THE STAGE: THE VAMPIRE AND THE STALKING VICTIM

CHAPTER 1. PARANOIA

You might call me paranoid. If you did, you wouldn't be the first and maybe it's true. Although, under the circumstances it's difficult to tell.

I thought the man sitting on the bench at the bus stop hiding his face behind a newspaper was him. I could have been wrong, of course, but I instinctively stepped out into the street and flagged down the first taxi cab I saw.

My heart raced as I leapt into the back seat. My throat felt like it was closing up as I hoarsely instructed the driver, who was already rejoining the stream of traffic, "Take me to 85th and Riverside, please!"

I carefully arranged my purse and briefcase on my lap as I always do, so I won't leave anything behind when I get out. As I did this, something caught my attention.

There, wedged in the crease of the seat was a playbill that a previous passenger must have left behind. In Victorian lettering surrounded by a scrolling border, it read, "Blood and Stilettos." Beneath this was the image of a man in a formal hat and theater cape embracing a woman in an open-shoulder dress, her hair cascading around her shoulders. Both were vampires and they were silhouetted against the background of a full moon. I was so intrigued by this image that I momentarily forgot my panic.

As I read the dates of the play's performance, I saw that one was scheduled for this evening. How I wished I had the luxury of attending. But, my life had become so frenzied these past few weeks. Ever since I broke up with my now ex-boyfriend, I had been besieged with all kinds of unwanted letters, gifts, e-mails and text messages. I kept hoping it would stop, but instead, his campaign of harassment was getting weirder every day.

Although I desperately needed a pleasant distraction, as soon as I arrived back at my hotel, which was more of a refuge than a home since I was forced to put most of my things into storage, my first task was going to be changing my cell phone number. I had already received about a dozen text messages from him today. That's down from the twenty-eight messages I received yesterday. And, of course, the day wasn't over yet.

Today's messages were more disturbing than previous ones. For instance, one of them read, "You look so hot in that green dress." This one was particularly panic-inducing because it made me think he had observed me at some point on my way into work. How else would he know I'm wearing a green dress?

Then, after a completely private, closed-door meeting with a colleague, I received another one that said,

"Dexter wants to share more than just a cup of coffee with you. Don't be naive!" This one baffled and disturbed me the most. How could he know about such a meeting unless he was at my office?

I questioned my co-workers. I told them I was having a problem and I asked if anyone had talked to or seen a man of his description anywhere in the lobby or around the building. But, no one had and most of them just shrugged off my concerns. Maybe they think it's just a small personal problem or that I'm being paranoid, but it seems pretty clear to me that he's watching me very closely.

Finally, the cab stopped at my destination. I paid the driver and, with a wishful thought, I stuffed the playbill for "Blood and Stilettos" into my purse and hastened into the lobby of the hotel. I was headed straight for the antiquated elevators when I heard someone call my name.

"Julia?" I turned to see the clerk waving an envelope. "I have a letter for you here," he said. Immediately, I could feel my anxiety rising.

I had checked into this particular residency hotel because it is for women only and represents a refuge to others like myself. It is staffed entirely by men who are all uniformly dark-complected with foreign accents, all very polite and, almost without exception, young and good-looking.

I was momentarily reassured by the humanity reflected in the sparkling eyes of the clerk as I took the envelope from his hand and thanked him.

Once the doors closed behind me, my apprehension seemed to rise with the elevator, increasing every second as I hastily tore open the envelope and read the enclosed note:

Dear Julia,

Stop being foolish and come home. You know I love you. We can work things out, if you will only meet me half way. You know my number. Call me. Let's talk.

Forever in love,

Terrence

I was disgusted, so much so that I felt like I was going to be sick and the lurching halt of the elevator as it arrived on my floor didn't help matters.

I fumbled for the key to my room, instinctively looking into all of the little recesses along the way down the hall for fear that I might encounter him lurking in the shadows. I told myself I was being ridiculous. This hotel has good security and no men are permitted outside the lobby area except those who work here. Despite this, I couldn't repress a chill as I approached the door to my room.

Once inside, I locked the door and, still feeling utterly absurd, I wedged a chair up against it and under the doorknob as I've seen it done in movies.

I threw the note into the desk drawer along with all the other cards and similar correspondence I had received from him. I kept these tucked inside a notebook I used to log as much of the unwanted contact, as possible. Each time I added another piece of evidence, I resolved that if things got any worse, I would go to the police.

Although, I wasn't exactly sure what I would tell them. So far, nothing in his correspondence had been directly threatening. I told him only once, without equivocation, that we were finished and I never wanted to see or hear from him, again. That seemed to me to be sufficient and, taking the advice of experts, I resolved not to make any further contact with him in the hope that he would eventually give up. "Ignore them and they'll eventually go away," said my sources.

I had, also, taken as many steps as I could to evade him. I hadn't told mutual friends and acquaintances where I had gone. I changed my e-mail address and closed all of my social networking accounts. Although, none of my precautions had prevented him from making contact, so far.

Feeling frustrated, I called my cell phone company and changed my number for the second time. After this was done, I wrote the new number down and placed it in my wallet so I could remember it. Then, I sat there on the bed feeling very angry as I recalled all of the crazy things he had done since the break up.

The reason I had to get away from him in the first place was his increasingly controlling behavior. Once again, he hadn't done anything really violent by most people's standards, although he had become increasingly aggressive. He had begun hiding my mail and telling little lies to my friends like I was too sick or busy to talk to them.

Then, there was a particular incident in which he painfully restrained and twisted my arms behind my back in an unprovoked rage, so that I feared what he might do next. In that moment, I thought he was going to hit me, so I told him exactly what would happen to him if he did. And, I knew it was a threat I would have to make good on if he decided to test me. The whole situation had become too dangerous. So, I waited until he went to work and I escaped like a fugitive to this residency hotel.

But, maybe I was exaggerating the entire experience. Did I really have a good reason to be afraid of him? Maybe I was over-reacting, like my co-workers seemed to think.

Although, I was becoming increasingly paranoid about my treatment at work, too. Since this whole problem started, I began to notice how conversations would stop suspiciously as soon as I entered the doorway. And, at least, once I was sure I overheard a couple of them talking about how "she is really turning into a mess." Again, it was probably my imagination.

I sat on the bed, looking at the tattered bouquets of flowers in the trash and revolving these thoughts in my mind when suddenly I remembered the intriguing playbill I had placed in my purse. *Why should I punish myself by staying in all night? Why should I make myself a prisoner because of one crazy man?*

And, in that instant, I decided to dress for the theater and go see what promised to be a nice, entertaining diversion.

What would be the right thing to wear to an off-off-Broadway play about vampires? I decided on a black lace dress with a red lining, a pair of strappy, black high-heels and my favorite full-length, black leather coat. It would be dark soon and I'd be hailing a cab right out in front of the hotel. I thought I might as well dress for the occasion and do so fearlessly.

I was so excited to be going to see a play! Even off-off-Broadway productions in New York are really good. Being able to see great live theater on a whim is one of the perks of living in the City that I've always really appreciated.

I resolved that tonight I would not be rattled by the harassment. I would forget all about it, if only for a couple of hours.

CHAPTER 2. THE STAGE

Night had already fallen by the time I hailed a cab for the theater. I don't know if it is rational or not, but there is something reassuring to me about the darkness, as if it is a cloak of protection from prying eyes. Still, I couldn't help being acutely observant of every man I saw, afraid that any one of them might be him. My imagination was in overdrive and while I was aware that I was doing it, I couldn't stop myself. I could no longer distinguish a reasonable fear from an unreasonable one.

The driver stopped in front of the theater and I hopped out. In my eager anticipation of enjoying the play, I redoubled my effort to forget all my worries. Mentally, I erected a wall around myself. On the periphery of my vision, I was aware of men moving about, but I made a concerted effort not to pay any attention to them, while reminding myself that they were probably not a threat.

Once inside the lobby, I hastened up three flights of stairs before reaching the theater, itself, which was small, intimate and dimly lit. The old, fold-out seats were covered in burgundy red velvet and the entire room was paneled in dark wood, making for a hypnotically relaxing environment. I seated myself in the middle of the front row where I had a perfectly balanced view of the stage.

I took a deep breath and exhaled, feeling all the binding residue of my troubles leave me. And, thus unburdened, I settled deep into my chair and scanned the audience more out of a sense of human curiosity than a need to satisfy myself that I hadn't been followed.

"See? Everything is perfectly fine," I said to myself reassuringly. I had just changed my cell phone number, so I should not be receiving calls from anyone, but I turned off the phone, anyway, just in case.

I glanced at the playbill, again, in eager anticipation and wondered if the play would be as good as it promised.

After a little while, the lights in the theater were darkened, so that all focus was on the stage. The curtain rose and the actors began to speak and move about, but I saw no one who looked like the handsome man on the playbill. I was disappointed by this, but still intrigued by the storyline in which a young, 19th-century woman becomes a vampire and lives a life on the stage as a dancer throughout the decades. She is pursued by different kinds of villains both because she is a dancer and a vampire.

To my delight, at the opening of the second act, the curtain drew back and there upon the stage in the shadows wrought by the spotlight stood the most gloriously handsome man! He was a dead ringer for the image on the program. At last! This is what I had come to see.

From that point forward my attention was rapt. I could not take my eyes off the actor who played the role of the vampire Vasco Valverde, whose eyes twinkled with warmth and wisdom under the stage lights. I was entranced as he glided across the stage with the grace of a dancer. I hung on every bit of dialogue, somehow comforted by the warm and breathy timbre of his voice. I checked the program to confirm his name, Sir Arthur Edward, which struck me as a fittingly distinguished and noble-sounding moniker.

I gasped when, at a dramatic point at the beginning of the third act, the vampire Vasco seized one of the villains and drained his blood to nearly the last drop before breaking his neck and letting him drop to the floor.

As the vampires took their blood-thirsty vengeance out on the villains in the story who relentlessly pursued them, I imagined myself in the role of the dancer, Tilly, awash in his love and at peace in his powerful embrace. For the nearly two hours that the play ran, in the refuge of my imagination, I was Tilly.

The final curtain went down and the actors all came out on stage to receive their well-earned applause. They had given such a convincing performance that I was relieved to see that they were all still alive at the end.

The entire audience was very appreciative and the applause was sustained as many people rose to their feet. I was among them, clapping my hands enthusiastically.

When the curtain closed for the very last time and my fellow theater-goers began to leave, I followed them with reluctance.

We all filtered down the steps and out into the street. So complete was my suspension of disbelief during the course of the play that only until I was out in the darkness, with strangers moving all around me, did I remember the reality of the peril I was in.

With a chill, it all came back to me. I fought to keep it from overwhelming me by trying to reason myself out of these oppressive feelings, but it didn't help that I had to walk nearly a block before I was able to spot a taxi and flag it down.

I slipped into the back seat, once gain feeling euphoric over the fabulous play I had just seen and reminding myself that I was in no immediate danger. I successfully persuaded myself that, in fact, I was probably in no danger whatsoever. In the comfort and shelter of the cab, my worries began to recede in favor of my pleasant memories of the play.

Then, I turned my cellphone back on and discovered a series of text messages from him!

"Did you have a good time?"

"That black dress you're wearing has always been my favorite."

"Call me, let's just talk one last time."

"Impossible!" I thought. How could he be sending messages to my phone when I just changed the number? I was panic-stricken. Most disturbing of all was the content of the messages, which, again, were such that I believed he must be following me because he accurately described my clothing and my activity for the evening.

Yet, I couldn't fathom how this was possible because while I had not been as vigilant as I was at other times, I had not seen him. Was it possible he was having someone else watch me? That thought was even more terrifying.

Once again, none of the messages involved overt threats or anything I felt I could take to the police. But, my sense of paranoia renewed and strengthened itself and I found myself eying passengers in adjacent cars and people walking on the street with suspicion as we paused at intersections.

It enraged me that I had escaped the violent clutches of this control freak, only to be subjected to this kind of terrorizing behavior, which was another form of control, but at a distance. In bewildered alarm, I scanned the streets for anyone who walked, moved or dressed like him. These probably irrational fears reached their height when I arrived in front of my hotel and was faced with having to leave the safety of the cab.

There was always that momentary pause outside the foyer before the clerk recognized me at the door and buzzed me in. I knew I was vulnerable to attack in just those few agonizing seconds. And, tonight it seemed like a very long time as my anxiety mounted. I was relieved when I heard the familiar sound of the buzzer and I hastily pushed on the door.

Once inside the quiet, empty lobby, I breathed a sigh of relief.

I hurried into the elevator and up to my room, locked the door and barricaded myself inside. Then, I turned the phone off for the night and went to bed.

In an attempt to calm down, I tried to focus only on the pleasant events of the evening. In my mind, I replayed the image of Sir Arthur Edward on the stage and his sensual and amazingly realistic performance as a vampire, sucking the blood from evil-doers. In my half-asleep reverie, I saw myself in his arms, resting under the moonlight, completely at peace. Finally, I relaxed entirely and drifted off to sleep.

For the next couple of weeks, I attended a performance of "Blood and Stilettos" every evening without fail. These were hours of calm and peace when my mind was emptied of every other thought. It was my respite from the fear I lived in most of the rest of the time.

When I was not attending the play, I worked and I worried about my stalker whose communications were becoming increasingly invasive. He continued to let me know that he knew where I was, what I was wearing and who I was talking to, even in completely private conversations.

This went on during work and after. I continued to find more messages after each attendance at the theater.

In frustration, I called my cell phone provider and told them of my dilemma and how I had changed my number, but to no avail. It was here that I experienced some good fortune because the person I happened to get on the phone this time was very knowledgeable. He asked me if my stalker had ever had my phone in his possession for even a minute.

I replied that he had.

I learned that stalking software could be downloaded on a cell phone in a matter of a minute or two, which would then allow a stalker to see you, know your location, intercept your phone and text messages and even allow them to hear conversations when the phone was turned off!

I thought of all the times that I had taken the phone with me under the most private circumstances, of all my angry outbursts against him when I was alone in my room and thought no one could hear and even the current conversation with my service provider. *Was he eavesdropping right now?* I was both dismayed and enraged!

"Isn't that illegal?" I asked.

"Yes. If you do it to someone's phone without their permission, it is."

"Should I go to the police?"

"You could, although there's no way to prove who put it on there," he said. "But, we can get it off right now by re-uploading your operating system."

I impulsively agreed to this plan, which wiped my phone's system clean. Then, I changed the number for the third time.

Later that same night, I attended the theater, again. I was scared to go out, of course, but I was scared all the time, anyway. So what was the difference? At least, there at the theater, I could free my mind from all of this stress for a little while. I sat on the front row, completely absorbed in the now familiar story. Most of all, I was enthralled by Sir Arthur Edward, himself.

When I rode home in the cab that night and turned my phone back on, I was relieved to see that there were no messages. In fact, after I had my phone's operating system re-uploaded, the creepy text messages finally stopped altogether, but afterward the nature and method of his communications changed and became more frightening. He began sending more letters, more flowers and other unwanted gifts.

He was very careful not to sign his name to any of this new correspondence as he had formerly done and it was typed and printed out, rather than being in his own handwriting. The tone of his messages changed, too. Instead of begging me to call him or see him, they began to take on a more menacing tone.

In one such piece of correspondence, which had been dropped off at the hotel, he wrote: "You will never be rid of me. I'm never going to leave you alone. If you change your number again, it won't stop me. If you move, I'll find you. I will follow you and when you least expect it, I'll be right behind you because I own you."

I felt completely isolated. I had tried to do all the right things. I listened to the advice of so-called experts. I kept records and I warned people at work that this was going on and tried to enlist their help, but no one seemed to take the problem seriously.

When the aggression in his messages began to escalate, I decided it was time to go to the police. If nothing else, I thought, maybe I could get some kind of advice or direction in how to deal with this problem.

I collected my journal, the notes and other evidence I had amassed, which was virtually amounted to an entire dossier, and took a cab to the local police precinct. But, the cops didn't believe that any of the evidence I gave them amounted to a bona fide threat and without a such a threat, they said, it was not stalking, at least, in the legal sense.

I asked about an order of protection against him, but they told me that wasn't a good idea because all he would have to do is take one out on me and have me arrested.

I didn't get any good advice from them, either. Furthermore, one of the cops suggested that I was probably allowing my imagination to runaway with me and I should just go home and forget about it.

Of course, none of this made me feel any better.

The only bright spot in my life was the theater. I continued to go every night. It was my sanctuary and if the cop was right about anything it was that my imagination was running away with me - it was running wild with thoughts of the actor who played the vampire.

When the stress of my situation got to be too much for me, I allowed myself to find an escape in this fantasy world.

My greatest release came at night. Although, I was often restless and had difficulty sleeping, I would tell myself that if something terrible happened in the night, I would have no control over it, anyway. And, although this wasn't a really comforting thought, it was a resigned one. And once I took my thoughts to this point, usually, in extreme exhaustion, I succumbed to sleep.

At these times, I would find solace in my recurring dreams of vampires and romantic love. It was a world of horror, but one without stalkers. It was one where I was free and in love. I was not looking over my shoulder. I was not responding to threats.

Often, I would be standing alone in a cemetery, surrounded by a nebulous fog and although it was dark and the wind blew dried leaves and rustled the foliage making a softly eerie howl, I was not afraid. I was perfectly still and at peace. I felt a strong awareness of everything around me, every scent and every tiny movement of an insect on the ground.

Then, a cloaked figure would emerge from the shadows of a tombstone and, as is common in my dreams, I could read his thoughts and I knew he could read mine.

He walked closer to me, turning his face toward the shimmering beam of light from the full moon as it pierced the branches of the trees. I found a strange comfort in his presence. I was magnetically drawn to him and as we moved closer to each other, I more vividly discerned the outline of his features, which were sharp and dignified like those of an ancient nobleman. He was a creature of preternatural beauty, a fusion of the vampire Vasco Valverde and the stage actor who played him.

In another moment, I was locked in his embrace, gazing longingly into his obsidian eyes as they reflected the moonlight. He moved to kiss me and I acquiesced. He caressed my shoulders, then my breasts as he nuzzled my neck. I was seduced, completely under his spell.

The dream always ended the same way. I would see his bared, wolf-like teeth just as he was about to sink them into my neck, but I always sprang back to consciousness right before the act was complete. Each time, I awakened flushed and strangely aroused.

Despite its dark nature, this dream was far from being frightening. Instead, it was a comfort to me. It was a pleasant diversion derived from my childish obsession with an actor. The memory of these dreams would stay with me and carry me through the cold drudgery of my day until I arrived at the theater, once again, for the next night's performance.

Is it possible to focus on some desire with such

intensity that we make it come true? Maybe I am giving myself too much credit by even wondering about such a thing. But, as I sat in my customary theater seat I began to imagine that Sir Arthur Edward noticed me.

Of course, it might have just been a coincidence that he cast a glance in my general direction once or twice during his performance.

Yet, something like this happened or, at least, I imagined it did on the following night, as well. After the show, I lingered as long as I could without feeling uncomfortable. It's not good to be the last person to leave a crowded room, especially when you have a stalker.

I was walking out close behind the crowd, which had grown progressively larger after each successive night's performance when, suddenly, I became aware of a presence behind me. I had that prickly feeling you get when you sense someone is looking at your back. In my over-excited condition, I turned around and automatically assumed a defensive stance.

I was relieved and pleasantly surprised to see Sir Arthur Edward standing behind me.

"Pardon me," he said, with all the courtesy I would have expected from the character he played on stage. "I couldn't help but notice that you've been here every night for the past two weeks. I wanted to thank you for your loyal patronage and support of our production."

"Oh!" I said, somewhat taken aback. He was devilishly handsome and radiated a sensual allure from beneath his stage make-up, which made his dark eyes seem to glow. "Yes, I've been enjoying the play very much."

"I'd love to hear what you like about it. If you could wait just a few minutes, we can go together for a cup of coffee. There's a little place around the corner."

"Sure," I said, as if in a dream. "I'd love to."

Blood on the Stage

We seated ourselves in a dimly lit corner of the cafe. Sir Arthur was dressed in an opera cloak with a large collar and a red silk lining. The quaint flair of this costume was amplified by his classical good looks and Gable-like charm.

We both ordered coffee, which was just the typical fare and far from extraordinary. I noticed that Sir Arthur hardly touched a drop of his.

We talked about the play at length. We discussed the writers, the costumes and the tightening up of the production from one night to the next as it became increasingly perfect. I talked about my obsession with the story and the realism of the actors' performances. Of course, I didn't mention my stalker, although the fear was on my mind and he must have picked up on this.

"Are you expecting someone," he asked.

"No," I replied. "Why?"

"You seem nervous. I see you looking around the room and starting every time the door opens."

I shifted nervously in my seat. I had become so accustomed to looking over my shoulder that it was second nature. I didn't even realize that I was doing it. "I have someone who seems to be stalking me," I admitted with reluctance.

"Stalking? Who is it?"

This was really embarrassing to admit. Having an ex-boyfriend stalker made me feel like an idiot because everybody I told about it either acted like I was exaggerating or making it up. But, I told him the truth about what was happening. In fact, I told him the entire story.

It was a relief to tell my story to someone who seemed to understand, who didn't call me paranoid or tell me I was probably just imagining things. In fact, he seemed to take it all very seriously. I wasn't used to this, at all, so I didn't know how to react.

We talked for a long time and eventually realized that the hour had grown very late. He saw me to a cab and we parted company. I looked into his eyes and longed to feel understood and safe for just a little longer. I wished for one whole day of happiness. When was the last time I had a whole day without some kind of terror in it? I couldn't remember.

When I got home that night, I was stunned to find that my room had been re-arranged. I might have thought it was the work of an over-zealous housekeeper, except for the unsigned note I found on my pillow.

It said, "If I ever catch you with another man, I will kill you both."

I can't tell you how horrified I was by all the implications of this event. How did he get past security? Non-employee men were not allowed on these upper floors. How did he get into my room? And, had he, in fact, been watching me at some time during the evening?

I couldn't make any sense of it. But, I knew there was no point in mentioning to anyone except maybe my new friend because I'd just be dismissed or called crazy.

The next day, I went to work as usual. I was there for a few hours before I was called into a private meeting with my immediate supervisor. He said my my work performance was not up to par and he was going to have to let me go. There was no warning about this, which is customary before an employee is fired. Instead, it came completely out of the blue. I was stunned. As far as I knew my work was as good as it ever was, if not better, because I had really thrown myself into any distraction I could find since this whole stalking nightmare began.

I thought about it afterward and I realized something important. All this time, I thought they didn't believe me, that they hadn't taken the danger I was in seriously. Now, I realized that they were afraid of him, too. They were afraid of what happens when a guy like Terrence goes to

Blood on the Stage

your work place and takes his rage out on everyone there trying to get to you. So, they fired me.

I didn't go back to my room. I couldn't face being alone there and the fear of what I might find. I felt safer where there were people. So, I lingered, sipping coffee for a long time at a nearby cafe until it was time to go to the theater.

Once there, I sat in my usual seat. There were more people in attendance this night than on any previous one. Out of habit, I scanned the crowd looking for threats. Finding none, I relaxed and prepared to enjoy the show. It wasn't until the lights had gone out and the curtain had gone up that I became aware of an unpleasant feeling, as if there were some unwholesome presence behind me.

Discreetly, I turned my head, ever so slightly, to look. There in the darkness, his face veiled by the shadows, I was certain I recognized Terrence!

I was terrified, absolutely paralyzed by fear! I couldn't move. I couldn't even breathe. I didn't dare turn my head, again, lest my worst fear should be confirmed.

At the end of the second act, I began to feel more at ease and barely turning my head, I noticed he was gone. Maybe he was never there at all, I thought. Or, maybe it was just someone who looked like him.

Momentarily, I heard the sound of a great tumult coming from backstage, which was uncharacteristic of any previous night's performance. It sounded as if heavy objects were being overturned and I fancied I heard l low menacing growls, as if an entire pack of wild dogs had managed to get backstage. A minute or so later, the curtain opened on the third act and without missing a beat, Sir Arthur Edward appeared on the stage, but instead of the usual actor for this scene, to my amazement, in his place I saw Terrence!

I watched with incredulity as Sir Arthur grabbed him by the throat, spoke his usual lines, tore open his throat and drained his blood. Then, he let him drop out of his powerful grasp to the floor of the stage where he lay, unmoving. When the curtain closed and reopened for the next scene, he was gone.

In stunned horror, I waited fairly disbelieving what I had seen. It must have been an illusion. Again, I looked for Terrence to be behind me in the darkness of the theater. As inconspicuously as possible, I turned to look over my shoulder, but no one was there.

Now, I was completely convinced that I had imagined the whole thing. After all, no none else in the audience seemed to notice anything unusual. Or, at least, if they had, no one gave any such indication.

As most of the audience wandered out of the theater, I lingered, waiting for Sir Arthur. We had plans to go out to a late night nook and I really did not want to go back to my room anytime soon. I wanted to stay out as long as possible.

When he emerged from his dressing room, I was anxious to talk, but in a low whisper he said, "Not here."

We hardly spoke a word to each other until we were seated in a dark corner of a late night lounge in the village. There was enough noise around us that we had to get very close to each to be heard.

That's when he confessed everything.

CHAPTER 3. THE CONFESSION

The extreme anxiety I had endured in the past weeks together with the illusion of the stage had conspired to bewilder me to the point that I no longer trusted my own eyes. Now, I couldn't believe my ears!

Sir Arthur divulged to me what really happened during this night's performance. My stalker had crept backstage between the second and third acts. He came up behind Sir Arthur and put his hands around his throat, but he was no match for the thespian. There was a scuffle involving the two of them and some of the other actors.

Less than a minute into the struggle and with time running out before the curtain was to go up, Sir Arthur dragged Terrence out onto the stage before the audience and incorporated him into the opening of the third act in place of the usual actor who plays the part.

I experienced different emotions as he explained this. I was still in a state of shocked disbelief, unable to fully comprehend his words. *Where is he, now? Is it really over? Or, will he be waiting for me in my room tonight, more angry than before?* These questions flashed through my mind. He must have read the confusion on my face.

"Don't worry," he assured me. "My colleagues are very old fashioned. They don't just drink blood, they consume flesh and clean the bones, as well."

"I beg your pardon?" I said. I'd heard of actors getting into their roles and transforming into their characters before, but this was ridiculous.

"We're vampires. The entire company of us," he said bluntly. "Sir Arthur Edward is only a stage name. My real name is Forneus Vanquo and I am a very old stage actor."

I shook my head involuntarily. I couldn't believe what I was hearing. I wasn't processing any of it very well on either an intellectual or emotional level. I could not grasp that my troubles with Terrence were over.

I still had a remnant of that fear within me, which had now become habitual. I couldn't suppress the worry, rational or not, that this wasn't really the end of my troubles.

Then, there was the notion of vampires performing on stage in New York City! This all seemed extremely unlikely to me at that moment. Although, I recalled how convincingly the actors played dead and how there was not even a slight movement of their chests from the involuntary act of breathing.

I, also, noticed that Sir Arthur had ordered a beverage, but he hadn't touched a drop of it, just like every other night we had been out.

Then, there was his appearance, which was as peculiar as it was fascinating. His eyes had a staring, hypnotic quality and his handsome features seemed to belong to another time. I considered that I'd never seen him without stage make-up, powder, rouge and eyeliner.

Furthermore, I'd never seen him in the daylight!

I thought I'd play along with this discussion, at any rate. There could see no point in being impertinent. If he thought he was a vampire, then that was his business and that was fine with me. After all, I knew people who thought they were witches, so what was the difference, really?

"How did you end up here?" I asked, after I regained some modicum of self-composure.

"My acting career began on the Italian stage," he said. "I was living in Italy in 1796 when a faction of Napoleon's army invaded. The secret of his reign of terror, which is never told in the history books, is that a great number of his soldiers were vampires. It was the vampirism running throughout their ranks that rendered them impervious to defeat. As soldiers, they were completely without fear and did their jobs with relish. It was during this siege that I was attacked by a legion of them during a performance of 'La Colomba Bianca.'"

I could hardly believe what I was hearing. But, I listened intently without interrupting this amazing story. And, he went on.

"We were only a company of actors, not soldiers. And, we were completely unprepared for so strange an occurrence, nor would I have believed such a fanciful superstition was a reality. Some years later, I re-invented myself on the London stage and lived there for many years under the name Sir Arthur Edward. And, now, I perform here in New York City in small independent productions like 'Blood and Stilettos.'"

There was something sincere about this bizarre claim and I was mostly persuaded that he was telling the truth. Although, another part of my mind still rebelled at the idea.

"Terrence is really gone?" I whispered aloud, half to myself and half to Sir Arthur.

I was so afraid and disgusted by him that the very name, Terrence, filled me with such horror and revulsion that saying aloud caused me extreme discomfort. This was the first time I'd been able to say his name since the worst of the terror had begun.

"Yes, I drank his blood and my colleagues picked his bones. They've taken the remains of his carcass to throw them off the Brooklyn Bridge tonight. He will trouble you more."

I was relieved to hear this re-confirmation. I couldn't help but feel a great weight had been lifted from my shoulders because, in my heart, I was convinced that he would have eventually killed me.

Yet, another cold terror struck at my mind. "What will happen when people realize he's gone? Will I become a suspect?" I asked.

"There's one thing you must remember - say nothing," he wisely said to me. "I was attacked and I acted in self-defense. You are innocent of any wrong-doing. Anyway, there was no other viable solution. You said, yourself, the police wouldn't help you. So, they are partly to blame for all of this."

"What if someone in the audience saw what really happened?"

"It's a play. No one would believe a man was murdered before their very eyes on the stage. They wouldn't believe it even if they were told outright. The human power to deny a terrible reality, even when it is right in front of them, is too great."

And, I knew these words to be all too true. After all, I was experiencing my own struggles with denial at this very moment.

It was almost too great a burden to bear to know that the world was not the way I had thought it was, all along. I was still reeling from this great shock. Nonetheless, I was certain that I had fallen in love with this man - or creature - whoever or whatever he really was.

After this evening, my life returned to more or less normal. Although, I still couldn't overcome the nagging sensation that something was wrong. I felt like some nebulous danger lurked around every corner. I shrugged it off to habit and I thought eventually it would wear off and I would go back to being a relatively happy, worry-free individual, again.

In fact, things were progressing in this direction. I felt like I was getting better, that my sense of safety was normalizing. But, then I received a visit from the police. They were just doing a little standard investigation about the disappearance of Terrence, they said. They assured me it was nothing to be concerned about, they just wanted to ask me a few questions.

I froze in terror. The police who had been no help to me when I feared for my life from this man were now clearly eying me with suspicion in his disappearance. I remembered Sir Arthur's admonition not to talk to them, so I said nothing. And, I tried to go on about my business, but I was very worried.

All of my earlier fears seemed to come down on top of me like an anvil dropping out of the clear blue sky. Suddenly I was a nervous wreck all over again. And, I was angry that I had been pushed into such a position. I had built up a lot of resentment toward the fact that I couldn't get help from the people who were supposed to offer the least little bit of support under such circumstances. But, most of all I was very, very afraid all the time - day and night!

Sophia diGregorio

CHAPTER 4. NEVERMORE

Because of all I had experienced, my sense of isolation was very strong. No one else besides Sir Arthur and his company of vampiric actors had ever acknowledge that I was in any danger or even pretended to care. By contrast, my co-workers, the police and anyone else I had told had not only brushed aside my very real concerns, but had gone on to create even more problems for me.

I had been treated very callously by the people to whom I had reached out to for help. And, when I needed them most, when they could have done the most basic, simple things to help me, instead they had turned their backs on me. They had called me crazy and a liar.

This feeling of having been victimized by everyone, including the police, had a stronger effect on me than the stalking itself. As a result of this entire experience, I now knew something I had not known before and which I had been far happier not knowing. I knew beyond the shadow of a doubt that I lived in a world full of people who lacked any empathy or compassion for others - a world full of monsters.

I soon moved out of my building and into another residency hotel in the city, but this didn't stop the police from tracking me down and trying to force me to talk to them. I continued to refuse them an interview. At the same time, I was afraid because I thought this would only arouse more suspicion. Of course, I was innocent. But, I knew that wouldn't matter to them.

One night after a performance, Sir Arthur and I went out to a night spot and had a few drinks - or, at least, I did. He could see that something was weighing very heavily on my mind. And, frankly, I was just plain scared of the world as I had come to know it. I asked if we could go somewhere quieter to talk. I didn't want to be here any longer and I didn't want to go home, either.

We left that place and wandered the dark, empty streets of the city. We walked on for some time until we were away from any other people.

Although, I was in the hands of a more than capable body guard, I still felt afraid. I couldn't rid myself of that habitual state of mind, which had virtually destroyed the happy life I once had.

I did not want to go on living with the constant nagging anxiety about what was around the corner or what might leap out from the shadows behind me. My biggest fear now was that the new boogie man would be sporting a badge.

I wanted this terror, which truthfully I had felt even before the stalking had begun, to finally end. I did not want to feel afraid of anyone, again.

I turned to him and asked, "Is there some place we could go to be completely alone?"

"What kind of place?"

"Where do you live?" I asked.

"In the churchyard," he said. "We could go there."

We turned our steps in that direction and soon passed through the old wrought iron gates, whereupon we stood in the midst of a very old tombstones and crypts. Some were so old that the names and dates had been worn completely away by the elements. I shuddered inwardly, although in the past few weeks, I had become strangely comfortable with a certain level of discomfort.

We walked between the tombstones and up to a large, white marble structure, embellished with figures of angels and demons.

There, we sat and talked for a while.

"Are you ever afraid of anything?" I asked him.

"I fear no man," he said.

"Not even the police? What if they learn the truth about Terrence?"

"They won't," he said emphatically. "It's too incredible."

"But, what if they do?" I asked, wringing my hands. "I stupidly went to them hoping they would help me. I wish I had never done it. Now, they're harassing me."

"Don't play their game," he said. "In fact, you don't even have to be in the game, if you don't want to. It's your choice."

"What do you mean by that?'"

"You could join us. Then, you'll stop being afraid. The dead are never wrongfully prosecuted."

I had already been thinking about this, almost from the moment I was convinced that he really was a vampire. In the back of my mind, I began to consider how to bring an end to my troubles once and for all. As it was, I was wholly alone in the world, surrounded by people whose minds I could no longer understand and who didn't seem to make an effort to understand me, either.

Sir Arthur was the first person who had listened to

me, who believed me and who had in any way come to my defense. And, I had come to believe that I loved him.

"Could you really make me like you are?" I asked. "I never want to be afraid, again. It's such a terrible feeling."

Without saying another word, he kissed me. Although, I was resolved to giving up my old life for a new one, I felt a deep sadness because my old life had been such a disappointment to me. I was overwhelmed by this heavy feeling, which came from the knowledge of being surrounded by so much wickedness in the world.

I succumbed to weeping. But, he wiped away my tears with his cape and asked me, "Are you sure this is what you want?"

I considered for a moment before answering. Then, I said, "Yes. I cannot go on living my life the way it has been, afraid of the cold, empty people all around me. Their unwillingness to look at reality and inability to empathize frightens me. At least, vampires are honest creatures who can accept the truth that is placed before them."

"Yes. Perhaps because it takes courage to face the truth and all who become vampires must face a horrible truth most people are too weak-minded to accept."

"I can accept the truth," I said in between sobs. "I have accepted it and I want to be fearless like you."

By this time, it was well past midnight under a full moon. There in the little churchyard cemetery, the night was still and the air had a clean, fresh smell as if it had never been touched by the city.

Sir Arthur Edward and I had been talking while sitting on top of one of the long raised tombs.

Once again, he asked me, "Are you absolutely sure?" and his voice had a low, solemn tone to it that I had never heard before.

"Yes," I said. "It's what I want."

As soon as I said this, he took my hand, we stood up and he led me to the chapel there in the churchyard. In the back of this old building was a little door. He opened it with an antique-looking key and we walked carefully down the uneven stone and mortar steps into the basement of the church, which was full of little tombs and piles of bones.

The air in here was considerably less fresh and wholesome. It was filled with the smell of decay and mold so strong that it burned my nose a little. My eyes were just beginning to adjust to the darkness when Sir Arthur struck a match and lit an old oil lamp that rested on a shelf. Shadows began to leap and dance upon the walls of the old charnel house.

He guided me to a worn sofa that sat in the corner, which might have been used by a caretaker who took naps while on the job. There he paused and helped me off with my coat. Then, he pulled me close to him just as in my dreams. I felt his cheek upon my cheek and I was trembling a little, although, I wasn't sure if it was out of nervousness or anticipation.

He began to kiss me, gently at first, before his passion gave way to a hunger. His kisses became more fervent as his tongue probed the depths of my mouth. After all that had happened, I was pleased to discover that I could still become aroused and I returned his kisses with equal intensity. Despite the damp chill, I felt my temperature begin to rise. My cheeks felt hot and suffused with blood.

Slowly, almost without my being entirely aware of it, he began removing my clothes. Once he had accomplished this purpose, he paused for a moment. I saw the flame in his eyes as he seemed to visually devour me, while caressing my waist and hips. I felt flattered by this. In return, I couldn't help but admire his nobleman's, stately good looks and for a moment, it seemed as if time had unwound itself and I was no longer a part of the modern century.

Then, he wrapped his heavy cloak across my shoulders and we descended as one onto the sofa.

As I had previously suspected, he had the powers of a mind reader. He seemed to know exactly what to do and where to kiss me to bring me to the utmost state of emotional and physical excitement. His hands were firm, but gentle and his touch had a slightly electrifying quality.

He lavished me with a profusion of kisses wherever it pleased him to do so. He prolonged this delight for a long time until I began to feel an excess of this pleasure, heightening all of the sensations in my body.

Then, he turned me in such a way upon the sofa in a way convenient to him and I felt his tongue, hot and probing. Sometimes he seemed to devour me all at once, gently nibbling here and there and sending an infusion of tingling pleasure upward.

I was like an initiate at the threshold of a sacred temple. Now, the door was flung wide open to me and Dionysus was invoked! He gave way to his carnal desires and was soon in a frenzied worship at the altar of passion.

Sensations of intense pleasure traveled up and down my limbs and great waves of heat passed through me, again and again, until I lay exhausted on the sofa feeling overwhelmed at the outpouring of love I had for this being who promised some hope to me in a world of darkness.

This sense of love and gratitude brought a smile to my face as I gazed upon the object of my devotion. Seeing this, he enfolded me in his arms and renewed his fervent kisses, just as when we first began.

I did not know if he loved me. But, at least if he did

not, he gave a good imitation of it and I vaguely wondered if the romantic revery I'd engaged in during the previous weeks had actually been a premonition. I did not linger on this thought for long as the throbbing distraction between us grew in intensity. He finally released it from its bondage. After which, he did the natural thing as he went on, kissing me and caressing me until he was overcome by his own passions. A torrent of warmth flooded over me again and again before the final crescendo of sensations came amid his own deep groans of pleasure.

This was not quite done and I was still experiencing the small spasms of delight when he enfolded me in his arms, once again. I could see in the dim light made by the old oil lamp that this face had changed. Although not entirely unpleasant, he looked fierce, as if he had lost all control during the previous act. His eyes were blood red and teeth were sharp and white.

I had little chance to consider this further before he applied his lips to the artery on my neck, sank his teeth in and begin to drink. I experienced an ecstasy more exquisite than any previous one. It was so intense that I briefly lost consciousness.

When I awoke, the moldy dankness of the charnel house didn't seem to bother me anymore and I could see in the darkness as well as if the sun was shining. I was aware of every little sound, every noise made by a cricket in a crevice of the foundation, screaming out his tune in the night. I felt a renewed strength and a peculiar hunger.

I looked into the eyes of Sir Arthur, again, and this time he looked normal. He took my hand and helped me to my feet and we walked out into into the night together.

At last, I stood fearlessly out into the cemetery feeling the streaming moonlight upon my skin. Only then, as I was surrounded in a shroud of nebulous fog amongst the tombstones, did I reflect on the fact that I had seen flashes of this night's events in my dreams.

I felt bold and fearless. And, from that moment forth I knew that I would be able to cope with whatever danger came my way. I was no longer in the game. I was out of reach and even if they did put their hands on me, they would not live to tell about it. I had transformed into a real life Tilly Rose, just like the dancer in the play.

I never returned to my hotel. I found myself more suited to sleeping in the privacy of a mausoleum, sometimes alone and at other times in the company of Sir Arthur.

Except that I lived at night and lost my taste for coffee, my life went on much as it had before the worst of my nightmare had begun. Although, I felt much more free. All disease and pain were, thereafter, unknown to me.

Now, I walk the streets at night alone - never with fear, but with anticipation of an attack that will provide me with sustenance.

I fear no man and I will nevermore.

BLOOD AND LINEN: THE VAMPIRE AND THE RUNAWAY WIFE

CHAPTER 1. THE OGRE

It's funny how we can travel down the road of life for quite a while, thinking everything is all right. Then, one day we wake up and discover that we have made a wrong turn a long distance back and there's no way to turn around. And, the only choices we have lead to a dead end. Like a rat in a maze, we can choose to go left or right, but either way we are still caught in the same trap.

That's what happened to me. It is how I came to be what I am and it's why I don't sleep at night, anymore.

Please, don't think that I'm telling this story just to get sympathy for myself or to justify the decision I made, which to you might seem immoral. I know that to a lot of people there is no justification for a wife to defy her husband, not according to the laws set forth by men and ascribed to God. According to these laws, it is a wife's duty to obey her husband. She is his property, body and soul.

And, I might have agreed with that once, myself. I might have said that it was wrong for a wife to look for affection outside of her marriage. I might have wondered why a woman would find it so difficult to remain faithful to her husband, whom she promised to love, honor and obey. I might have said there was never any justification for such a thing. But, I was naive. I didn't know what marriage meant or what isolation, abuse and privation could do to a woman.

Mine is a cautionary tale. I do not expect sympathy. I know I will not find it. But, maybe my story will save some poor soul from similar torture.

When I think about it, which I do from time to time, I am amazed at how we, as women, have not come a long way, baby. I'm amazed at the tyrannical fraud and sham that is represented by modern marriage laws, which might make good subject matter for a Gothic horror novel set in sixteenth century Italy, where a woman is held captive by dagger-wielding ruffians. Yet, this is not sixteenth century Italy. It is the United States of America in the twenty-first century, but little else has changed.

And, unlike a character in a Gothic novel, I was not a poor orphan or a damsel in distress. I was a well-educated, independent, modern woman. I committed myself to a long-term relationship relatively late in life and I thought I had done so carefully. I asked my family and friends what they thought of him and they all agreed he seemed like a good, decent person.

Although, his family was not as well-off, our level of education was equal and according to the sociologists, psychologists and other experts who tell people what kind of match they should make, we were a likely couple. We had common interests and I was happy for a while.

Blood and Linen

I never wanted to marry in the legal sense. But, he did and he insisted on it. One day, he surprised me by driving me to the courthouse and, once there, presenting me with a ring. I did not want to sign the papers and I protested loudly about it. Disturbingly, no one at the courthouse found anything odd in any of this, although, I was very angry, sobbing, loudly protesting and even ran for the door to try to escape, at which point he grabbed by roughly by the arm and drew me back.

The papers were signed. It was done. And, nothing seemed out of the ordinary for a little while.

There are many other people who will attest to the fact that a couple can enjoy a very happy relationship for a long time up until the point where they sign a marriage contract. After this point, one member of the party becomes tyrannical. It is like the transformation of a changeling in an evil fairy tale. It was at this point that the man I thought was my trusted friend became the ogre - the betrayer.

It wasn't noticeable in the first few days or even weeks because the transformation took place so gradually. Over time, he became increasingly perverse and demanding. And, when he didn't get his way, he would throw terrifying tantrums, storming about the house and committing violent acts on inanimate objects.

He began to delight in humiliating me in different ways. Although, I was obviously horrified by the things he did, he would only laugh. It seemed to me he had ceased to respect me as another human being, but I didn't know what to do about it. I only hoped it wouldn't get any worse.

Now, of course, there are some old-fashioned people who would say it is a wife's duty to perform her marital duties any time a husband demands it. They say there is no such thing as a man forcing a wife against her will within the bond of holy matrimony. But, surely even the most zealous among them would see that reasonable exceptions should be made for circumstances of prolonged or life-threatening illness. Or, simply, when a wife is tired from having worked ten hours per day to support her husband.

As part of his grand scheme for complete domination of me, he insisted on having complete control of my sexuality. He said my body belonged only to him and I was not permitted to place my hands in certain places on myself, even while I was at rest. At any time while I was relaxed or while I was working on something, he would launch an assault on me. I would not be released until he was done molesting me, which he did, laughing like a demon all the while.

His delight in sadistic perversion seemed to grow, day after day, week after week as he immersed himself in a variety of pornographic films. As these abuses escalated, he grew increasingly wary of other people. He began to lie and manipulate even our closest friends and family members. I was not permitted to be alone with anyone or to have a conversation on the telephone unmonitored by him. I was allowed to talk to no one - not a man nor a woman - without him being present.

If I happened to be on the phone and no one else was in the room, he would come in while I was in no position to resist and begin performing some revolting act on me against my will. When I tried to get away from him or get him to stop, he only persisted all the more. He was a huge man and there was no escaping his grasp for me. And, the more he laughed at his assaults on me, the more he disgusted me.

I could not understand what had happened to my friend, the person I had trusted most in the world. "Hate" is not a strong enough word for what I felt for him, now. I loathed him and I wanted him to go away.

As I became increasingly resistant to his assaults, his

carnal appetite seemed to accelerate beyond reason - or, at least, what seemed reasonable to me. And, it came to the point that I could not pass near him without him tearing my clothes off me and assaulting me with the brutality of a wild gorilla.

He would grab my arms and pull at my clothing and when I tried to pull away from him, he would become more aggressive. Then, he would grab me around my waist or pull me by my feet and violently force himself on me, sadistically laughing all the while. This began to happen two to three times per day.

Frequently, he would lunge at me from behind while I was cooking dinner. It is amazing how a man of his gigantic stature could sneak across the room so quietly, but he did. On one occasion, he grabbed me from behind, turned me upside down by my ankles and assaulted me in a violent manner, although he was careful never to leave any visible bruises. I had the presence of mind during the course of his perverse assault to try to reason with him. I tried pleading with him to stop. But, he would not stop until he had finished his business.

He was sometimes amused and sometimes completely unconcerned by the effects his actions had on me. He never showed any remorse for his unwarranted violence and the situation was only getting worse, his attacks were becoming more frequent and more violent. He was completely unresponsive to my pleas for mercy and my attempts to reason him out of his aggression.

I learned that I could not talk or reason him out of his violence. Nothing deterred him. Once, after a particularly brutal and unexpected attack, I asked him, point blank, why he had done it. He simply said, "Because I wanted to."

I had never known him before to be so callous or without conscience. But, it was clear to me that once he had coerced me into signing that infernal marriage contract, he had assumed the right of ownership over me. I could only conclude that the person I thought I knew didn't exist and never really had. It had all been an act designed to lull me into a sense of trust, so he could take advantage of me every way he could think of, including financially.

In the matter of just a year, he had managed to plunge me deeply in debt. He had taken control of my property without assuming any responsibility for it, because my name and only mine was on everything we owned.

I could handle the brutal violence, I thought, but not the damage to my finances and my financial reputation. It was then that I became determined to do something, although, I wasn't sure what.

While these horrors were taking place, I survived by imagining that I would someday live my life as a free person, again. I dreamed that one day, I would be able to go out for coffee with friends or see my family again, and there would be no one to stop me. I would be able to wear attractive clothing without the fear of being assaulted by the ogre. I would be able to move about or converse unmonitored and unmolested. As things were, I was not even permitted to drive my own car anywhere without him, not even to the grocery store, nor could I carry on a phone conversation without him listening in.

I envisioned a new life - a fearless, perhaps even reckless life, where I was in complete control of my own sexuality. It would be one where I owned my own body again, as I had unwittingly signed my rights to it away in the courthouse when I signed a contract with The Devil, himself.

In anticipation of this moment, when I would one day, again, be free, I had collected a few items and secreted them away where they would not be found. I had a collection of, as yet, unworn lacy thongs, garter belts, sexy dresses and shoes. When no one was looking I would look at these things and imagine my life as I wanted it to be.

One night, after another vile, sweaty session against my will, when the smelly, barbarous traitor who had all but destroyed my life had finally gone to sleep, I lay wide awake involuntarily contemplating the horror and misery of my circumstances.

While I knew I could not leave because of legal and financial obligations, I, also, knew that I couldn't stay in the same room with him for another minute.

For the sake of what was left of my sanity, I had to get out of here!

I crept carefully from between the white linen sheets and tip-toed down the hallway. Then, I took some items from my secret stash of sexy clothes and put them on.

I remember admiring myself in the mirror as I put the black lace stockings on, sticking my toes into the end and pulling them up one at a time. How good they felt on my legs! Because of the ogre, I hadn't dared to wear anything like this in years! And, I was filled with a sense of adventure and, dare I say, my own sexual power, which, if only for this moment, I was sole owner of.

Gazing into the mirror, I paused for a moment and, as a small act of defiance, I touched myself in a way that I thought seemed very bold and I watched myself in the mirror for a few moments, inwardly smiling at my own moxie.

Then, I put on the red lace thong I'd been saving. I fastened the old-fashioned garter belt around my waist and attached it to the stockings.

I had purchased a matching red push-up bra, to match the thong. After putting it on, I pulled a choker-style necklace of polished garnets from my little jewelry box and placed it around my neck. This was the finishing touch. I paused to admire myself, once again.

Considering all I had been through, I thought I didn't look too bad.

Finally, I put on a tightly-fitting, black dress of the knit variety, which clings in all the right places and is very flattering to the figure.

I attended to hair and make-up with a feeling of happiness I had not experienced in years. It was wonderful to apply powder and rouge for my own pleasure with my own thoughts in mind instead of fear and anxiety. Although, these latter emotions still lingered, I pushed them aside for the moment.

I reassured myself that the ogre still slept. Then, I took my purse and shoes in one hand and the car keys in the other and quietly went out the door.

I put the car in neutral and let it roll down the slight decline, out of the driveway and onto the street. Then, I started the engine and drove out of the cul-de-sac before daring to turn on the headlights.

I feared the consequences if he awoke and discovered I had escaped. It would be an affront to his sense of power and control over me, which was sure to increase his violent mania. But, for now, I was free, even if only for a few hours.

CHAPTER 2. INTO THE NIGHT

I had no idea where I was going to go. The hour was already very late.

I drove without purpose, without any destination whatsoever in mind. Simply being behind the wheel of a car gave me a renewed sense of being in control of something in my life. It was a pleasure just to drive and to see the city after dark, which was full of other people moving about freely.

As I drove the streets at night, I admired the mundane, everyday things, which during the course of my imprisonment, I had nearly forgotten. I was thrilled at the sight of the light emitted from ordinary street lamps as it reflected off the shiny, black asphalt. Even the red, green and yellow of a common traffic light held for me a particular brilliance and beauty that night, as if it were somehow more vibrant than before.

I wondered at these little things and in what seemed like a short time, I reached the edge of town. There, I found myself surrounded by darkness, except for the beams of my own car's headlights, which dimly illuminated the roadway and the shadowy limbs of the surrounding trees.

I entered a road that I don't recall ever noticing before and followed the winding, narrow roadway to its end, which was at the zenith of a tall hill that afforded me a view of the city. There, I cut the engine and sat for a few moments in quiet contemplation, watching the cars move on the grid of streets in the valley down below.

Now that I was free, I had brief thoughts of driving to Mexico and never coming back, again. But, these were only fleeting thoughts borne on surges of sheer panic, which rippled through my entire body whenever I thought of having to return home. I did not want to go home. But, the reality was I had responsibilities, which I could not run from, even though facing them meant subjecting my body and mind to further abuses.

I could think of no way out. I could turn left or right, but I was still stuck like a rat in a trap.

Reluctantly, I started the engine and slowly wound back down the hill.

Somewhere in the darkness, I must have taken a wrong turn and when I finally came back out to the place where I thought I had come in, the road looked a little different. In fact, it looked cleaner, newer and the asphalt was much blacker than I had remembered.

But, I thought little of it until I realized that if the town was, in fact, behind me, I was driving away from it and there was no place on the narrow highway to turn around. To my further dismay, it seemed that the highway had only one lane, which went in only one direction. But, this was impossible!

I drove on for some distance, but still I recognized nothing. There were no familiar houses, other buildings or landmarks. I saw no signs. There were no gas stations or convenience stores. There were no other cars, either in front of me or behind me. There was nothing but the gnarled limbs of trees reaching outward and the seemingly endless flat, black asphalt of the highway.

As I drove on into the night, I began to feel increasingly unnerved. I tried to tell myself there was no reason to feel anxious. After all, this was just a road like any other in the country, a secondary or tertiary highway, which would eventually intersect with another one and, at that point, indicate how far away I was from any nearby town. And, then I would have my bearings, again.

Nonetheless, I drove in a state of increasing anxiety for several miles without seeing even so much as a mile marker. In desperation, I was about to do something dangerous and illegal in the form of a dramatic U-turn, which would have me driving in the wrong direction at night on a one-way road, when I suddenly recognized the clear signs of human activity straight ahead.

In the approaching distance, I saw lights and what looked, at first, like a large house with a lot of cars parked in front of it. As I drew nearer, I saw that it was not a residence, but a bar, aptly named, "The Dead End Saloon," because it was, in fact, situated at the abrupt termination of the highway.

The parking lot was quiet. I saw no other people and was in no fear as I got out of my car. As I walked to the front door of the establishment, I happened to take notice of the other cars along the way - all of them high-end luxury models of German or Italian manufacture. This detail seemed at odds with the remote, if not pastoral, setting I found myself in.

I wasn't wearing a watch and I didn't take note of the time before I got out of the car, but I knew it had to be past the hour state laws permitted the sale of alcohol. So, I reasoned this was one of those afterhours clubs I had only heard about, where the owners have a license to stay open past the designated hour, as long as they do not serve liquor.

I was wholly unprepared for what I saw when I pushed open the front door. It opened into a luxuriously decorated and expensively furnished vestibule, whereupon I was greeted by a tall, gaunt, older man attired in a black tuxedo and white gloves.

It was if I had entered a dream. He welcomed me to walk into the main room of the establishment, which was full of well-dress patrons. At the far end, a lounge singer crooned while caressing the keyboard of a large piano. Two heavy curtains were drawn up on either side of the stage, which complemented the gold and scarlet decor of the room.

Patrons sat in well-stuffed chairs surrounding little tables, each adorned with a single candle. The lighting was a dull, reddish tinged kind that gave a garish glow to the entire room and everything in it.

I took the room and all its contents in as if in a single snapshot in my mind. In fact, it was somewhat a blur and, in retrospect, there were important details I might have missed. Had I taken note of these things, I might have turned and fled at that very moment. But, I did not.

Instead, I took a deep breath and walked over the bar to order a drink so that, at the very least, I would not be standing alone in the doorway with no apparent purpose.

I took possession of an empty bar stool and in a matter of seconds a man, who was dressed very much like a magician of the variety who are known for their waving of wands and pulling of rabbits out of top hats, appeared in front of me. I was taken aback, not only by his outlandish costume, but by the unearthly beauty of his face. I felt that I had stared at him far too long to be considered polite, but I could not take my eyes off his remarkable features.

"Would you care for a drink?" he asked.

This was a simple question. Why couldn't I answer?

Blood and Linen

I was mesmerized, drawn in by his eyes, which held the sparkling fascination of rare gemstones. His face was a study in masculine beauty from the sensual fullness of his lips to the sharp lines of his nose and the exquisite angles of his jaw. This was made all the more intriguing by the shadows produced by the flickering flame of the candles sitting on the bar, which played upon his ivory skin to a dramatic effect.

I was conscious of an awkward pause and I knew that I had held his gaze is a way that might easily be construed as flirtation. In an effort to disengage myself from my own imagination, which had already begun to run wild with dark fantasies, I spoke. Although, it was a monumental effort to say anything, at all.

"Yes, please," I said. And, those simple, common, ordinary words sounded forced and awkward to my own ears.

"What would you like?" he asked, smiling. It was a knowing smile, as if to say he was well aware of what I was thinking.

"What would you recommend?" I responded, still struggling to maintain a sense of decorum because the one thing that was inexplicably running through my mind was that I wanted to feel the arms of this mysterious man around me. I wanted to know what it felt like to have his body pressing against mine, as if doing so would somehow free me.

"We have a selection of fine wines. Perhaps you would like to choose from among them?" he said and, for the first time, I realized he had a slight foreign accent, which only served to heighten my sense of curiosity and deepen my attraction to him.

"Would you mind selecting one for me?" I asked. I was really in no condition to make a decision, even about the most trivial matter.

"Of course," he said. Then, he disappeared from my

view behind the row of patrons at the bar.

I turned and gazed out upon the room, once again. This time I was more attentive to details and it occurred to me that I was not in a legal establishment. This thought filled me with terror because I am not the kind of person to break the law, even those laws I find arbitrary and absurd. I remembered with alarm that it was far too late for the dispensing of alcohol to be legal and he had just offered me a glass of wine!

This point soon receded to minor significance in relation to the entire scheme of things, as I observed a couple disrobing each other with their teeth while standing at a baccarat table.

I was somewhat shocked at the blatant public display of sensuality and the obvious arousal of the man of the couple whose member was causing his tight pants to stretch dangerously close to the point of bursting as it swelled and bulged. Although, he didn't seem to take notice of this embarrassing state of affairs as he was intently lapping his tongue at the top of her nearly bursting corset top.

This startling spectacle engaged my attention for a few moments until I realized that a similar event was taking place at the neighboring table. This fact distressed me, yet I noted that no one else in the room seemed to be the least bit concerned. In fact, as my gaze penetrated the smoke and shadows, I discerned a veritable orgy of illicit activities on open display.

I watched as a very beautiful woman with long, black wavy hair down to her tiny waist, fully nude except for a pair of high heels, tottered along amid the crowd of people completely unmolested. This was not a liberty I enjoyed while fully clothed in my own home! And, yet here she was moving fearlessly among apparent libertines engaged in all manner of perverse persuasions.

What had I stumbled into? A nudist colony? A swing

club, perhaps? I had no idea. I had only heard of such things.

Yet, I thought, it must be something like that. In every corner of the room, there were couples, sometimes threesomes, their tongues caressing bare skin while their hands and fingers massaged hither and thither.

When I allowed my vision to blur a little bit, to take in the scene all at once, I perceived that the entire room was in a state of perpetual motion. Some movements were slow and sensual, some fast and purposeful. And, it appeared as if the room was arranged to allow for some dark, private recesses for those who preferred a little more privacy and more openly placed groupings for those who enjoyed an audience.

As I focused in on a nearby couple, I thought I saw something far more bizarre, although, at the time I attributed it to the phantasms of my imagination. Captivated, I watched a man rapturously kissing the nape of a woman's neck. At first, he seemed to nibble at her earlobes, which elicited some giggling. Then, he moved his lips down and when he had placed them over the spot where her artery might be, I'd have sworn I saw him plunge his teeth in, at which moment she appeared to go limp in sheer ecstasy, while he hungrily sucked at her neck.

The whole scene of the room was like something Brueghel the Elder might have painted on canvas, depicting perverse sixteenth century Flemish peasants, only this was far more strange. Why I had not seen it before, I do not know. As I said, I would not have stayed for a moment had I noticed it, at first. But, now, as I sat there taking it all in, I felt some incongruous sense of peace. I did not feel threatened by any of what I saw because it wasn't happening to me. Furthermore, it appeared that all of the people involved were willing participants and no one was being forced to do anything against his or her will.

When the flamboyant bartender returned, I turned my gaze back upon his handsome face and accepted the glass of red wine he placed before me.

I thanked him and then I asked the question I most wanted an answer to, "What kind of place is this?"

He smiled like a crocodile and said, "It's my place. It's a place of dreams where people live out their greatest desires and fantasies. Here, even the darkest of your secret wishes can come true."

I thought I knew what he meant by that. Although, I was sure I had wandered into some kind of brothel. Whatever it was, it didn't sound entirely legal to me. I paused for a moment before I asked my next question because I didn't want it to be taken the wrong way. But, out of concern for my safety, I had to ask, "What about the police?"

"What about them?" he asked.

"Well, aren't you worried about doing something that might be considered illegal?" I stammered, in spite of my best efforts to speak smoothly and clearly.

"If you look around, you'll see more than one officer of the law is here tonight enjoying himself to his heart's content," he said, pointing to a couple at the end of the bar, one of whom was still dressed in uniform.

Clearly, I was in the shadow of the beast and there is no safer place than that. Thus reassured, I said to him, "Well, it's a beautiful place," and, as if to punctuate my words, I raised my glass and took a sip of the wine.

"This is only a small part of it," he said. "Would you like to see the rest?"

"Yes," I said. In fact, I relished the idea of a personally guided tour. I had seen enough here and I was eager to be alone with this mysterious man who had awakened something in me that I had long ago forgotten, if I ever knew it at all.

Blood and Linen

With the grace of a ballroom dancer, he stepped around the bar to where I was seated and giving me his hand. He assisted me as I descended from the bar stool.

He guided me through the crowd and we emerged into another even larger, although, less densely occupied room. Here were a few couples engaged in various stages of copulation on sofas arranged near beautiful Roman style statues. The centerpiece of this room was a square-shaped hot tub, made of what looked like illuminated alabaster, with stairs descending into the water from all four sides.

We wandered from this room into a yet larger one where there were four classical nude figures and exotic, tropical plants surrounding a very large swimming pool, which led from one room to another.

What appeared from the exterior to be just a little saloon was, in fact, a mansion of rooms, each designed for pleasure, each more beautiful than the previous one.

After he had shown me several of these rooms, I began to wonder how such a magnificent establishment managed to escape my attention all this time. I asked, "Why have I never seen or heard of this place before?"

And, my mysterious tour guide gave an equally mysterious answer. He said, "The Dead End Saloon can only be found under extraordinary circumstances. So, a better question might be, 'What brought you here tonight?'"

"I don't understand," I said. And, I truly did not, although I was trying very hard to absorb his meaning.

"Perhaps you have had some trauma or some dramatic shift in your thinking tonight, which brought out some unusually profound desire. It is a compelling desire of one kind or another which brings people to my door."

Of course, I knew the answer to that question. This momentary insight he seemed to have into my very soul brought such a sense of relief to me that I nearly broke down in tears. It was as if he could read my mind. Indeed, something extraordinary had happened tonight. I had made the decision to break free from a terrible prison.

I told him about my husband and the abuses I was suffering at his hands. I don't remember the words I used, only that they flowed very passionately from my lips. I explained how I had set out from the house in an attempt to escape from him, if only for a few hours, although I might be made to pay for it later. But, I had some how gotten lost and ended up on the one-way road that led here to this place.

When I had finished telling my story, he smiled in a way I found both alluring and frightening at the same time.

"Tell me," he said, "If you could have any desire fulfilled right now, in this moment, what would it be?"

I looked at him in all of his strange beauty, surrounded by the magnificence of this last room we had entered, which I only now realized was a huge bedroom fit for a wealthy sheik. It was arrayed in pink and gold with a splendid, silk-draped canopied bed situated in the center.

"I want to be free," I said.

And, as I looked into the dark, piercing eyes of this elegant stranger, I knew in my heart he had the power to free me, although, I was uncertain at that particular moment just what that power was.

Even if it were to be something terrible, I thought it could not be worse than the fate that awaited me when I returned home, which I could no longer endure.

CHAPTER 3. THE DEAD END

I had spent years in a marriage where I was abused and humiliated, deprived of any real human affection or consensual conjugal union. This poverty of any real love or even empathy had seared a deep scar upon my soul. In my isolation, which in marriage was the worst sense of loneliness I had ever before experienced, the hunger for a real oneness with another being grew to such proportions that I felt I had lost all control.

Finding myself with this mysterious man, in a situation full of possibilities of things that could be, I felt the greatest longing for freedom from the bondage I had suffered for so long. I truly believed he had the power to set me free, after all, it was my desire to be free that had driven me here, in the first place.

The room seemed to have grown dark except for the faint, flickering incandescence given off by several large candles surrounding the bed. It was there that we seemed to be magnetically drawn as one.

Sliding his arm under my body, he drew me gently

toward him. I was pleased by the firm, muscular hardness of his slender body. Although he was not a large man, he possessed a calm, gentle strength, which served to soothe my rattled nerves. He gazed into my eyes and I seemed to fall under a spell of tranquility. Presently, I was aware of nothing but the gentle compression of his lips against mine.

Momentarily my mind drew back to reality and the absurdity of this entire situation flashed into my mind as I realized I was here alone in a strange bed with a man I had only just met but minutes ago. Yet, I could not linger long on this perfectly rational thought, before being carried away again by the seemingly preternatural beauty of this creature whose face was now bent over mine, kissing my lips and ardently caressing my tongue with his.

After lavishing my lips with a profusion of fervent kisses, he slipped my dress off over my head and suddenly I was there in my bra, stockings and little else. I might have felt vulnerable, but I did not because I knew that whatever was about to take place here would be my choice. If I wanted to leave, I was free to do so. If I wanted him to stop doing something he would stop. I knew that if I said, "No," my autonomy would be respected. I was free to give my consent and free to withdraw it without fear of violence.

I reclined on the bed in anticipation. The pillow softly received my head and he began kissing me, partially liberating me from the encumbrance of the remaining clothing. He seemed to devour me with his eyes before he began kissing, stroking and applying his lips wherever he pleased. He proceeded on in this way until, with some impatience, he removed the last impediment of garments, altogether. Once this was done, he kissed me with a passion bordering on savagery. All the while he stroked the sides of my abdomen, his hands eventually wandering down to caress the insides of my thighs.

All at once, I felt my face flush red with heat. It seemed to me that the cause of this was more than just the novelty of being with a very desirable, new lover. Rather, it was a subconscious realization of my bold rebellion. I was here with a man who was not my lawful husband. It was dangerous and forbidden, although, consciously, I never for a moment considered it be wrong. After all, I owned myself - I and no one else - and I would decide when, where and with whom I would have sexual relations. Nonetheless, my cheeks were as hot as a flame, spitefully betraying my inner shame.

But, there was little time to dwell on this idea because now my lover's hands sought further intimacy. He pulled my red, lace thong down, to which I gave willing assent by moving my hips to allow this action to take place. Here he lingered kissing, stroking and probing with his tongue until I threw my arms over my head, overcome by pleasure and lay writhing and moaning in ecstasy.

I was so distracted by my own pleasure that I did not take note of when he had removed his own clothes. I only recall seeing him lying there kissing and caressing me, the flame of the candle reflecting of his black hair and imparting a sense of warmth to the ivory pallor of his skin. As I gazed at him, it occurred to me that he had an ambiguous, ageless quality. He seemed at once fragile and strong, his pale, sinewy limbs and narrow waist belonged to a very young man. But, the centuries of wisdom in his eyes told another story, altogether.

My mysterious lover paused and allowed me to recover a little before resuming his lovemaking with renewed vigor. Awash with long-contained desire, I welcomed him with urgency and I was distantly aware that an involuntary cry of rapture escaped my lips at that moment. My desire for him grew until I felt a powerful throbbing, which I could not be sure was from his body or my own. This culmination of our mutual gratification thrilled through us both for what seemed like a remarkably long time before we collapsed in the afterglow of our lovemaking.

What did it mean to have such harmony with a complete stranger? I had not been with many men before the dreadful ogre. How could this be? Was this true love? I did not know.

With wonder, I looked deeply into his eyes. I did not trust own mind not to be given to dark fantasies and so it was unclear to me if what I saw was real or only the fantastic product of my traumatized psyche. What I saw in this moment should have terrified me, yet it did not because years of abuse at the hands of my husband had caused me to lose my sense of rational fear.

My newly-found lover's eyes appeared to me as endless, black holes and as he bared his teeth like a salivating wolf, a look of brute viciousness spread across his face. Yet, I was not the least bit frightened.

In a moment of passionate savagery, he sank his teeth into my neck. Still, I was not afraid. There was no pain, only pleasure as my entire body thrilled with an ecstasy previously unknown to me. Momentarily, I was aware of the warmth draining from my body. Slowly, and steadily like water flows out of a sieve, it drained away into the darkness. I remember nothing but complete and utter blackness.

In what could have only been seconds later, I was awake and conscious. I hadn't felt so well in a long time. Minor aches and pains seemed to have vanished and I felt utterly renewed.

I kissed my new lover, whose face had resumed its former grace and beauty, remembering the glorious love we had just shared. Encircled in his embrace, I was aware only of the feel of his body and the vaguely spicy scent that emanated from his skin. He brought me back to the full awareness of myself with his words.

"You're free!" he said. "You can do whatever you want now, but you must remember you are one of us - a Child of the Blessed Death. You are free to go and free to return at will." He smiled in a way that was at once charming and cadaverous.

Suddenly, as if a hypnotist had snapped his fingers, I became fully conscious and aware of who I was and what I was doing there. A small shock of panic jolted my senses. "What time is it?" I asked.

"It is very late, but do not worry. There is time enough. Perhaps you should go home and sort a few things out before you come to visit me, again," he said.

"Yes," I said. "I must do that," although the merest thought of returning home filled me with dread. "I will try to return to you, but what if I can't find my way?"

"You will find the way here," he said reassuringly. "You must only desire to come here, again, and you will."

That seemed a little cryptic to me, but I had no time to argue about it. So, I asked to be shown out and escorted to my car.

With dawn soon approaching, I returned home. I cannot rationally account for the means by which I arrived back at my house. The strange highway led out as surely as it had led in, with no sign posts and no markers. Ahead of me, I saw the familiar lights of the city and I breathed a sigh of relief.

With reluctance, I entered the bedroom and slipped back in between the familiar, plain linen sheets, as if nothing unusual had happened. I reflected on my nocturnal adventures as I allowed the darkness of the room to envelop me. All the world seemed silent and at peace.

I was desirous of sleep and a succession of images of

pianists, card players, dancing ladies and other garish and marvelously grotesque scenes lured me into a deep repose. My dreams were filled with fantastic images of flickering candle flames and shadowy phantasms dancing on the walls.

As dawn broke and the first hint of light began to stream between the crevices of the window shade, I slowly began to awaken. Presently, I became aware of the loathsome ogre who lay beside me, rousing from his long night's sleep. His foul morning stench permeated the room and curled in my nostrils. I was filled with disgust.

In a state of half-consciousness, he turned his body over and laid his huge, heavy hand with the palm downward upon my abdomen and squeezed me painfully. This was another unpleasant habit of his in which he persisted, despite my having asked him repeatedly not to do that because of the excruciating pain it caused me.

But, of course, he didn't care. Rather, he delighted in inflicting pain on me. It was his reassurance that he was in control, that he had total power over me.

In the eroding darkness, he moved his slimy lips up to my face, leaving dribbles of his sticky, putrid saliva on my cheek. It was the same routine every morning. I knew he would soon be on top of me, crushing me and I would be immobilized in pain while he ritualistically took his vile liberties with my body.

I was seized with anxiety, but I dared not move a muscle. As this nervous tension grew within me, my fear grew to great proportions. I had tasted freedom only hours ago. Was I not free? Had it all been a dream?

With these thoughts, I was instantly filled with uncontrolled rage at this injustice. I would not endure being violated ever again!

I could feel the muscular contractions in my face and I

was aware that my expression must have taken on a very angrily contorted appearance. Instinctively, I bared my teeth at him, I even fancied I heard a low growl emanating from deep in my throat. It seemed an involuntary act on my part, almost as if I had been possessed by a large, carnivorous beast. I didn't feel at all like myself. In my own mind, I was now the perpetrator and he was my victim.

In that instant, he stopped what he was doing. As he looked into my eyes, he appeared to be seized by some invisible force, which could only be the spirit of terror, itself.

He stared at me with an expression of pure, unadulterated fear. A cry of horrified alarm escaped his lips, which had gone pale and gray. His face took on a strained appearance and all the veins in his neck swelled as if under insurmountable pressure. His entire body shook and his heart raced for what might have been a couple of minutes before it ceased to beat, altogether. Finally, the pupils of his eyes dilated.

Presently, my tormentor died. An expression of abject terror remained permanently frozen upon his face.

I watched the effects of his shock with amazement. Did I cause this?

The coroner's report concluded his death was due to natural causes, apparently, cardiac arrest. I was legally free and entirely above suspicion.

They say nothing is more final than death. Although, on a more personal note, I have found this to be both a great truth and a profound fallacy.

What is completely true is that once you have begun to traverse certain roads, there is no turning back. You can only go forward.

I have found a new life of renewed passion in death. Mine is the life of the undead, which is monstrous, but better than a life of human enslavement to a tyrant, which is no life at all.

BLOOD AND BLACK LACE: THE VAMPIRE AND THE CALL GIRL

CHAPTER 1

Classified Ad - Personals

"A Message to Count Malpheus: Someone dear to you is in grave danger. To keep your promise, call 555-0198. Hurry! It is a matter of life and death."

Date: Nov. 13, 20--

To Whom it May Concern:

I am writing this letter to you in order to set straight certain facts of an affair, which recently played out publicly in the newspaper and has caused some confusion, especially among those who may be acquainted with the people involved in the drama.

You may have seen the above personal ad, which ran for a week in the classified section of the paper. Maybe you read it with passing curiosity, never imagining it pertained to someone you personally know and care about. It is to you, especially her family and closest friends, I am writing this letter in order to inform you of the truth about her fate.

It is a story you will not read in the newspapers or see on the nightly news. But, it is the whole truth as I know it to be so. I am not affixing my name to this letter for reasons, which will undoubtedly become clear to you as you read further. It concerns a woman, thirty-five years of age with long, wavy, chestnut brown hair and striking green eyes named Erika, whose body inexplicably disappeared from the city morgue.

She was a kind, decent person and a life-long friend of mine, who despised lies and secrets. She didn't keep them well except where discretion was required to protect other people. And, while some of what I have to say in this letter is graphic, I say it with her unreserved blessing. She would want you to know the truth, however shocking and bizarre it is.

I do not remember the first time I ever met Erika because it seemed like she was always there. We played together as children. She was always precociously self-confident. She lived her life with remarkable zest, truly exercising her own will in all matters, regardless of social convention or public opinion.

Maybe it is true that we come into this world with our personalities already formed. It was certainly true in Erika's case that her sense of self and force of character seemed to have been in place very early on.

Even as a small child, I never knew her to be shy or unwilling to express an opinion, especially when she felt very strongly about something. At times, she could be showy, even flamboyant. She was a natural performer and was happiest when she had the attention of every pair of eyes in the room.

In high school, Erika wasn't like the rest of us girls who were uncertain, if not a little afraid of boys. She was always the adventurous one. Although we gossiped and giggled about her sexual exploits and were sometimes shocked by her risqué deeds, we all secretly admired her boldness.

She dared to do things the rest of us would never even dream of trying. For example, on one of those dull days when students had been called down to the gymnasium for an assembly, she sneaked away to make out with one of the class bad boys in the janitor's closet. Of course, she got caught and spent a couple of weeks in detention for it, but she didn't care.

Another time, she managed to create a little private time with her beau of the moment by pulling the fire alarm, prompting an evacuation of the entire school. We all stood outside wondering what was going on while the two of them made the most of their opportunity behind the stage of the school theater. This act resulted in a long suspension, but she remained undeterred.

Somewhere along the way, Erika developed a taste for the finer things in life, despite her fairly average, lower-middle class upbringing. On the other hand, it may have been because of this that she always wanted more out of life than the average life usually brings.

She was never satisfied with the common or the mundane. When she did something, she did it all the way. She studied French and Russian and eventually achieved a Master's Degree in the latter. She taught Russian at the university for a while, but didn't stay at it because she had too much integrity to go along with the system. She just couldn't stand the mediocrity or the politics.

Afterward, she made a success of herself in

commercial real estate until the market crashed. If you live in the city, odds are you've seen Erika's face on billboards or in real estate magazines at one time or another.

Ultimately, the one thing she was highly successful at, which afforded her the luxurious lifestyle she had dreamed of since we were kids, was her outcall work.

It's no secret to anyone who knew her well and the only reason she ever kept it from anyone at all was her antipathy to the foolishness and intolerance the subject aroused in some people. As I said, it was never a big secret, however, I suppose there were those who wondered how, even after the mortgage crisis was in full swing and real estate hit the skids, she was able to afford designer clothes and that red, convertible Mercedes she was so fond of.

Most people go with the flow, whatever that is. It is an unusual person who dares to break out of the box and live her life the way she really wants to despite prejudicial judgments and established social norms. This was Erika. Although, where her personal life was concerned, she was not the type to break a lot of taboos, at least, not like some people might imagine, however, her professional life was another matter.

Her client list was comprised of a lot of wealthy men, including politicians and celebrities, many of whom were secretly transvestites and fetishists. But, there were, also, some who just need an attractive woman to take to events, one who would form no romantic attachments or expect anything beyond a cash payment. Erika was particular about whom she took on as a client. But, the one thing they all had in common was they were men with lots of money, many of whom she had culled from her real estate business.

She was as careful as anyone could be under the circumstances. She didn't get into situations she didn't think she could get out of and just in case she miscalculated, she packed heat.

While she enjoyed the money and felt genuine gratitude toward her clients, she harbored a deep disdain for them. Of course, they didn't know this. But, believe me, I knew. Erika was a good actress when she needed to be, but the rest of the time, she didn't hide her feelings about anything.

She liked to brag about how she made big money fast. Among her favorite clients were the much older ones who were lightning fast. A really old guy might pay for half an hour, but be all done in five minutes and she would be clutching six Franklins, wearing a big smile on her face as she watched him close the door on his way out.

Clients who wanted companionship were a lot more work. She had to incorporate different elements of her personality into these transactions. For them, she was partly a psychologist and partly a pretend girlfriend. These were the guys who sometimes paid $2,000 for one or two hours.

Such clients were more sophisticated and had more complex needs. They had fertile imaginations, but they were, also, realistic about the fact that they were paying for the services of a make-believe girlfriend. I had the impression they really appreciated her services from a practical standpoint. For the big players, a couple thousand dollars here and there for attractive companionship is a better deal than paying for a real girlfriend or a wife. It's a matter of economics.

Interestingly, an inordinate number of her clients who were sexual submissives were, also, hard-working, high-earning attorneys and judges. I learned from Erika about people in the legal profession and their love of being urinated on, spat at and whipped into a frenzy. She had a theory about why so many of them like to dress in women's clothes and be beaten. It was deep-seated guilt, she said. And, she was happy to oblige them. "There's nothing in the world more gratifying than taking money from a lawyer, then chaining him up to a rack and beating his ass," she once said with a sardonic laugh.

I was her friend and I knew what made her tick: Money. It's a universal need in the world as we all know it. It's why we leave our homes and go to some other place away from our families for several hours a day. It was her primary motivation in life; in fact, I think she may have been far more driven by the desire for money than most of us are. Some people are just like that.

But, I've never pretended to understand what motivated her clients to engage in their bizarre sexual behaviors. Some of the things they did were so strange that they would never be thought of as sexual by the average person, but, they were very sexual to them.

When she told me about them, I just listened. Sometimes I remarked with surprise or amusement. I was always careful about not saying anything to appear judgmental or patronizing, although I did worry about her safety. And, regardless of their wealth and standing in the community, I've always regarded her clients - many of whom are household names! - as degenerates and aberrations.

She collectively referred to them as "a bunch of sick fucks."

I, also, frequently heard her remark that right when she thought she'd seen it all, something else would come along to up the ante.

As it happened, I was there the night she got the strangest call of her life!

CHAPTER 2

We were sitting around one late afternoon at her condo, just watching a movie, sipping coffee and trying to relax when her cell phone rang. She remarked that she didn't recognize the area code, but she answered it, anyway.

"Hello," she said. There was a pause. "Yes, this is she." A pause. "Who did you say made the recommendation...?" She looked confused and there was another short pause. "That'll be $2,000 for two hours, paid up front" she said. She opened a drawer at her desk, extracted a pen and paper and scratched out a note while she listened. "Tonight? I don't know." Another longer pause. "Well, all right. When can I expect him?" And, then she hung up the phone.

"What was that all about?" I asked, remote control in hand. It sounded to me like I was going to be watching the rest of this movie on my own.

"That was a guy with a weird foreign accent. I wrote the name down as I understood it." She read from her note, "Count Malpheus." She put the note down and went hurriedly into the bedroom. "He said I came highly recommended by somebody whose name sounds familiar, but I can't quite remember who it is." She came back out with a dress, a pair of black lace stockings and a garter belt in hand to change into there in the living room, where we could better converse and added, "I'm sorry, but I just can't turn this down. I gave him my rate and when I sounded reluctant about doing it tonight, he doubled my fee."

I raised my eyebrows in silent assent at the statement. It was a lot of money for just a couple of hours.

"Would you mind feeding, Arlo?"

Arlo was her little Pomeranian. "No problem," I said.

"This guy sounds all right, but could you stay handy in case I need you for something? I've got my cell phone here," she said, slipping it into her purse, "and I'll call you, if I need you. I should be back in three or four hours, at most."

"Sure. What should I tell Jack?" I asked.

"Don't tell him anything if you can help it. You shouldn't have to deal with him, at all. I'll be back before it gets very late."

I hoped she was right. I'd be lying if I said I wasn't worried about her, but I tried to be supportive. She left the spare key to the Mercedes on the kitchen counter for me just in case I needed to come and get her.

I watched her from the window above as she went down to meet the highly-polished, black limousine that pulled up outside. The driver was an oddity. He might have been a little person or a dwarf, he tottered slightly from right to left as he walked around the car and opened the door for Erika. His attire had a classic flair and was topped off by an old-fashioned chauffeur's hat and white gloves.

I tried to take note of the license plate as he drove

away, but I didn't see one. This worried me a little.

Then, I waited on pins and needles. I paced the floor for a few minutes, wishing I could have somehow stopped her from going, but, of course, I had no power to do that. She was an adult - and a streetwise one, too, I reminded myself.

I talked myself into sitting down and soon I was absorbed in the movie again. When it was over, I checked the clock. About an hour had passed since Erika had left. I put in another movie. My attempts to relax were so successful that I actually fell asleep.

I awoke to the sound of a key in the lock of the door. The room was dark except for the solid, blue light emanating from the blank television screen. The sound of heavy, booted footsteps coming toward me on the kitchen floor told me someone was home, but it wasn't Erika.

It was Jack. Despite Erika's plan to the contrary, there he was and now I had to deal with him.

Jack was the typical kind of loser musician who commonly affix themselves to sexually available, financially powerful women like Erika. He was hot. Even I thought so. I always had to work hard to keep my eyes off his slender, wiry body and his lionesque, golden mane, which he was constantly struggling to keep out of those perfect, almond-shaped, blue eyes with their long eyelashes.

But, he didn't have much of a purpose beyond the ornamental. His only real achievement was mastering that one signature riff on his Les Paul and landing a job as the lead guitarist for a regionally popular rock band. Erika was by far the best thing that ever happened to him.

In the beginning, she really liked him. She still did, but, he had grown increasingly possessive and controlling. She was not unaware of this problem; I just don't think she felt it had reached the proportions where she needed to do something about it and she hoped it never would. But, from where I stood, he was showing increasing signs that he could become dangerous, if he felt anything threatened their relationship.

I know he wasn't very fond of me - not that I had done anything specific to lose his favor. But, no doubt, he feared any criticism I might make of him to Erika when he was not around. Again, this was something which I tried to refrain from doing. Besides that, he was jealous of any time Erika and I spent together, which he was not a part of and, therefore, felt excluded from.

The biggest red flag I saw was his desire to completely dominate her time combined with his expectation that she would financially support him. It seemed to me that he wanted the money she earned, but he didn't want her to actually go out and earn it because, by doing so, she was spending time away from him.

Jack had no real source of income of his own apart from the pittance he earned from the band's gigs and, most of the time, the boys either drank their wages away or were flat out paid in beer. So, he was always finding ways to wheedle a few hundred bucks out of Erika here or there, whenever he could. I remember her making a remark about it under her breath one day, after she had handed him yet another wad of cash. "It's like he thinks my pussy is his personal ATM machine!" she said. But, she kept on handing the money over, anyway.

"Hey," he said in his low voice, which had an adolescent, vaguely gravely quality to it despite his twenty-three or so years of age. "Are you awake?"

I was, but I don't think I was the person he was expecting. "It's me," I said.

"Oh," he said, flatly. "Where's Erika?"

"I don't know," I said. That was the truth. "What time is it?" *It had to be after midnight!*

Blood and Black Lace

"It's just after three," he said coming closer and flipping on the floor lamp near the sofa. He smelled of beer and cigarettes at a strength which can only be accumulated by spending several hours at a night club.

"After three?" I repeated in alarm. I looked around the room, but there was no sign of Erika having returned, no purse or keys.

"Yeah," he said, "Where is she?"

"She stepped out a little while ago, but she was supposed to be back by now."

"When did she leave?"

"It was still daylight," I recalled, "probably right around 7:30."

"Where did she go?"

He was asking a lot of questions for a guy I wasn't supposed to have to deal with. I was scared to tell him very much because Erika had told me not to say anything, but, at the same time, I was worried about her. I wanted to tell him what I knew so we could put our heads together.

"She had an unexpected call. It was a high-paying one, so she took it. But, she expected to be gone for only three or four hours, which means she should have been here three hours ago. She was supposed to call me if there was a problem." I checked my phone, but there were no calls. I checked her house phone, but there was nothing.

"Her car is still here," he observed.

"The guy sent a limo," I said.

"Where did they go?"

"I don't know. She didn't tell me. I don't think she knew."

"You're kidding!"

I just looked at him and slightly shook my head from side to side.

"Fuck!" he said.

Sophia diGregorio

I felt frustrated, too. "Let's just think for a second," I said. "Here! I'm going to call her."

Ring after ring was followed by a voice mail recording. *Nothing!*

We sent text messages: "Where are you?" and "Are you okay?"

But, these received no reply.

I was worried - frantic, in fact. And, I had no idea what to do.

Jack was disconsolate. His solution was to down a few beers and within the hour, he was out cold in the recliner. I tried to sleep on the sofa, but that was impossible.

When daylight pierced the windows and Jack roused from his self-medicated slumber, his mood had shifted from worried to enraged. He was angry that she would do this to him! Where was she? Who was she fucking? Why was she fucking him? What kind of idiot had a whore for a girlfriend, anyway? Why didn't she have a normal job?

Some of the things he said sounded almost rational to me because I felt the same way about it. I always felt that her career choice as a call girl was ultimately going to be a death sentence, but I didn't know what to do about it.

He said, "I never know what she's doing. I don't know if she's dead or alive, if she's coming home or not. It's all the time! I can't take it anymore. I just can't!" And, he slammed the door so violently it shook the walls and he walked out.

I can't tell you how worried I was. I felt ill. I thought my chest was going to burst from the anxiety. I alternated pacing the floor and frantically looking out the window. I don't know how long I was in this state, but it was daylight when I happened to see the black limo pull up outside. The odd little driver hopped out and graciously opened the passenger door.

Out stepped Erika smiling broadly, much to my relief.

Moments later, she was at the door, surprised to find that I had already unlocked it and was waiting for her.

"Oh! You're still here," she said nonchalantly. Apparently, she had no idea what kind of emotional roller coaster I had been on all night.

"Yeah," I said, trying to sound casual. "I was worried about you. I haven't really had any sleep yet."

"I told you there was no reason to worry, didn't I? It's nice that you did, but it was completely unnecessary."

"Well," I said, "I'm not the only one."

"Jack!" she said. "I forgot about him. He was here?"

"Oh, yeah!" I nodded.

"What did you tell him?"

"As little as possible, but, at the same time - everything I knew," I confessed. "I'm sorry. But, we were both worried."

"It's all right," she said. "I really don't care what he thinks or what he does, anymore."

I wondered if she had set me up, in a way. Maybe this was her way of telling him to get lost without actually having to say it. It's a classic break-up strategy, disregard a guy's feelings until he finally gets tired of being rejected, willfully gives up and goes in search of greener pastures. It makes it all seem like it was his own idea.

"So, what happened?" I asked anxiously. I was beyond exhausted, but I wanted to hear her story.

"Well, I thought this call was going to be unusual, but I was expecting the *usual* kind of unusual, if you know what I mean. Like, maybe he was into some weird fantasy role-playing thing where he's Mrs. Claus and I'm one of the elves. Or, maybe he likes to be bull whipped while covered in chocolate pudding, hanging upside down in the closet. That would be normal unusual," she said. "But, this was a completely different kind of unusual"

"How so?"

"Did you see the driver?" she asked.

"Yes, I did. He looked a little strange to me."

"Yeah, he was strange and very quiet. Honestly, I don't think he's human. I thought I was hallucinating, but, at one point last night, it seemed as if the limo was being driven by no one at all or maybe just some kind of spirit. He didn't say a word beyond necessary politeness and when he did speak his voice was weird, more like the croaking of a frog."

I didn't know what to say about that. I just chalked it up to imagination, of course.

Then, she said to me, "You know I never trust anyone who is too quiet. They're always hiding something. The driver and all of the Count's staff were extremely quiet. That was the first thing I noticed and it made me feel uneasy, but now, as I'm trying to sort it all out, I think these are simply very, old-fashioned servants. They seem to recognize the Count's authority, not just a as a boss, but like he's real royalty and they are conscious of their place. I've seen plenty of chauffeurs, valets, butlers and maids, but I've never before seen any who exhibited such servile deference to their employer."

"That's interesting, all right," I said. Actually, it wasn't particularly and I wasn't sure what she was driving at.

"But, now," she continued, "as I pull the entire experience together, I realize that they must be as old as the Count, himself. They must all be..."

"Be what?" I asked.

"I'm getting ahead of myself," she said. "I'll start at the beginning, otherwise, this isn't going to make any sense to you. It barely makes sense to me and I was there."

"All right," I urged, although I was exhausted. "Begin at the beginning. What happened once you arrived at his place?"

"A woman came out to greet me. She was strange, too

- tall, deathly pale and silent. I walked through the door, which is so wide and heavy that it has to have some kind of mechanism to assist in moving it. I was immediately taken aback - stunned, really - by the immense size of the room I found myself in. There was the Baroque-style furniture, the gorgeous paintings and the magnificent sculptures! And, then I was taken into another room by the lady and I realized that I had been standing in a mere vestibule by comparison."

"This second room was monstrously huge and glorious beyond all belief. The fireplace was large enough for several people to stand in and everywhere I looked I saw ornate carvings of all kinds of animals, flowers and little ugly creatures - I think they're called grotesques. The ceilings were high and the walls were windowless. There was only one huge chandelier in the room, emitting a soft, incandescent light from above and the fragrant scent of spices filled the air."

"I barely had the chance to take all of this in when I saw the most incredibly gorgeous man standing on the staircase, almost right next to me. I hadn't noticed him before, but, somehow there he was, tall, dressed in black, his dark eyebrows arching sharply over piercing, black eyes. I thought I had seen him somewhere before, although, at the same time I knew I hadn't. Yet, everything about him from his long, slender, pale hands to his full, sensual lips - even the way he moved, was all so familiar to me."

"At first, he made me a little nervous...," she said, pausing with such an expression that it appeared to me as though she were looking far away into the distance and seeing something I could not.

"Why?" I coaxed.

"Well, first of all, the guy is obviously very rich and powerful. I've never seen a spread like his. I mean the grounds were spectacular; the house looked like a modern castle. You know, it had none of the fortifications, but all of the style with its turrets and huge vaulted doors and windows. I was nervous because as a general rule, the more money and power they have, the freakier they are."

"But, the other thing was something he said," she continued. "Apparently, he told a little white lie about receiving a recommendation. He admitted that he had actually just seen my picture on a billboard. Some of my real estate advertisements are still around, you know. I didn't like the fact that he lied, but then...," she paused and her face took on a faraway look, again, as if she were suddenly remembering something very vividly.

"Then, what?" I prodded in an effort to bring her attention back to the present moment.

"He paid me," she said. "And, then he said he would double the figure, yet again, if I would have dinner with him. You know I don't turn down money or a good meal," she said smiling. "And, this was a feast, but he just sat and watched while I ate. I felt a little awkward because he kept staring at me the entire time as if he were studying me."

"That is strange," I chimed in by way of encouragement.

"Yes, very," she said. "And what's worse was I kept having the sensation that he was looking right through me, as if he could read my mind. Seven small courses came and went and he watched me eat while he asked questions, which seemed like typical small talk. But, there was more to it."

"What did he ask you?"

"He wanted to know where I was born and when. He asked me if I knew anything about my ancestry and if I had any children. I guess these aren't really unusual or particularly prying questions, however, they are a little unusual coming from a client, especially one who is

Blood and Black Lace

paying $8,000. It's not the kind of thing they're usually interested in. Normal questions from a client are like, 'Are you bi?' or "Do you do anal?' *That's* the kind of questions they ask when they ask anything, at all."

"So, what was this guy's thing?" I asked.

"Well, at first, I thought he was just going to be into some kind of elaborate role playing," she said. Then, she pulled back her hair so I could see her neck. "Look at this," she said.

"Oh, my god!" I cried. I was horrified at what I saw. There were two deep puncture marks on her neck, apparently made by some kind of large animal. The area around the wound was red and swollen as if it might be infected. "Should I take you to the hospital?"

"It's all right," she said casually.

"Does it hurt? It looks infected."

"No. It doesn't really hurt. I mean I can feel it, but it's no big deal," she said.

"How did this happen? Maybe we should put something on it, at least. Do you have any tea tree oil or antibiotic ointment?" I was headed to the bathroom to find a bandage, but, she stopped me.

"Relax," she said. "It's okay. Really!"

What else could I do? I sat down and tried to do as she said and relax.

"Listen," she said. "This guy isn't like a normal person."

"Yeah, that's pretty obvious," I said, sarcastically.

"No, I mean he's not like a regular guy, at all. He knows things. Like, he knows things about me that nobody else knows. There's no way anybody could know."

"Maybe he's been doing some research on the internet," I suggested. "You know, you can find out all kinds of things about people by pushing a few buttons these days."

"No," she said. "Not things like that. It's as if he knows my soul."

"If it's not too personal," I said, "how exactly did you end up with that festering wound on your neck?"

"He bit me," she said matter-of-factly.

I tried to suppress my alarm, as she continued speaking dreamily.

"He believes we were married once. He says I'm his wife from centuries ago," she said and her eyes took on that faraway look, again. "It's a crazy idea; I know it is. But, he's made me believe it's possible."

"How can that be?" I asked. "I've heard of past lives and there is some pretty compelling evidence for the idea that some people have lived before, but what could he have possibly said to convince you of something that sounds so insane?"

"It's not so much the things he said, really. Although, when he describes his home in Romania in the fifteenth century, I know somehow I've been there. I know every stone along the path in the garden. I can name all of the servants in the castle. I know which is the fastest horse in the stable. I can smell the flowers and the trees. The air is so much different! The swans that swim on the pond are as familiar as the back of my hand and when I peer into the reflection of the water, I can see myself in it and I *am* the Countess."

I didn't want to tell her how crazy I thought this whole thing was. I didn't think it would be right. She seemed to believe it so sincerely, but I wondered what this man had done to make her so willing to accept such obvious nonsense.

"Please, tell me more precisely, how *exactly* did you end up with that terrible bite mark?" I asked, again.

"It was surreal," she said, as if she were recounting a dream. "After dinner, we retired to another room and talked for a very long time. That's when he told me all of these things about Romania and our life together. He called me by the name, 'Carmilla.' Whenever I tried to correct him, he insisted it was my name. Once he could see that I was beginning to understand this idea - as absurd as it seems on the surface - and that I was beginning to feel that I really was his long lost wife, he took me into his arms."

"It was the most natural act of love I can ever recall experiencing, simply to be held by him. I remember looking up into his eyes. A wisp of his long, black hair touched my face and it seemed so familiar. Despite myself, I said the words, 'I love you,' and he kissed me with a passion I could only describe as a kind of hunger."

"We kissed for a very long time, almost frozen in this embrace. I could feel his swelling hardness pressing against me until it became a wild throbbing. When the intensity became nearly unbearable, he picked me up and carried me to a broad sofa."

"He went on kissing me, lowering his head to my neck and shoulders, lingering there for some time as he gently pulled my black lace thong aside. I barely noticed he was doing it because I was only aware of the heat of his lips on my skin."

"Before I knew it, he was kissing the insides of my thighs. It was all like a dream! I was aware of his lips and tongue probing and kissing me and before I knew what happened I felt a gush of warmth and and a thrill went throughout my body over and over again for what seemed an impossible length of time."

"It was a few moments before I recovered myself and caught my breath. Then, he was kissing my neck. It was pure ecstasy. I felt transported, as if I were in another place and time." She paused her speech. "And, then he bit me," she repeated, flatly.

Despite my efforts to remain open minded, I must have been wearing an expression of horror when she this. It's certainly what I was feeling, at the time.

"It didn't hurt at all," she explained. "In fact, I'd call the sensation erotic. And, then, he said to me, 'We will be together forever. After you are bitten three times, you will become one of us. You will be immortal!'"

She looked directly at me, right into my eyes, as she said, "It's my choice, he said. I have to decide."

Then she paused as she studied my face and added, "You don't believe me, do you?"

"I do," I said.

I lied. Of course, I didn't believe her. Can you blame me for that?

CHAPTER 3

In the following days, it seemed to me she had become obsessed with Count Malpheus, his vast wealth and his promises of immortality.

It is a terrifying thing to watch a close friend descend into apparent madness. You feel like you're losing your own grip on reality, as well. I told myself it was a passing thing, only a harmless fantasy.

She planned to see him, again, a few nights later.

A few days passed as she tried to decide what to do. She was torn between the life she was living now, which, truth told, was meaningless and full of melancholy in between the thrills of fast cash, and the dreams of a far better life, painted by Count Malpheus.

Meanwhile, she had to deal with Jack. I was there for one of his phone calls. It seemed to me that he was far from being done with their relationship, despite his assertions that he never wanted to see her face, again.

She held the phone away from her ear as he screamed, "You lying whore! Who do you think you are? Do you know how many women are waiting in line to fuck me? You've made a big mistake, bitch!" And, so on.

He didn't make any specific threats, at least, there was nothing we could take to the police, but it was all very unsettling. Erika didn't internalize any of his rhetoric, she just thought he was blowing off steam and hoped he would eventually skulk off.

She kept her second appointment with Count Malpheus.

The morning afterward, she gave me another intimate account of her evening with him over the phone. She found him to be wildly romantic and charming, not only because of his vast wealth and his dark good looks, but her sense that they were somehow soul mates, destined to be together for all eternity.

She had consented to a second bite, she told me.

At this point, I still thought it was all fairly harmless, or, at least, no more harmful than any of her usual activities.

Things were about to change drastically, though.

Later, on that same night, someone came into Erika's apartment and tore it to shreds. Everything was destroyed or defaced with obscenities. Some of her things were missing and she was stabbed several times with a butcher knife from her own kitchen drawer.

She was lying on the living room floor and near death's door when I found her. I don't know how long she had been there like that, but the scene was a bloodbath and she was white with the loss of blood. I immediately called 911.

Erika now lay dying in the hospital. I didn't have time to figure out what had happened. I couldn't think about that while she was in danger of dying at any moment. That fear overshadowed everything else.

I went into her room. I held her hand. And, with the little breath she had left in her body, she begged me to

Blood and Black Lace

find Count Malpheus. She knew she was dying and she said he was the only one who could help her.

"Who did this to you?" I asked.

But, she was too weak to give a reply and slipped back into unconsciousness.

Of course, I knew it was Jack. He was the one with the motive and he had said some things that sounded a lot like threats to me. I told the police about this. They questioned Jack, but he had a credible alibi backed up by the boys in the band, so they let him go. They figured that Erika knew a lot of people and the perpetrator could be any one of them. Besides, in the cops' book, prostitutes have it coming, anyway.

Her black book was missing from her apartment, which was now an official crime scene. The cops referenced a few of the names on her phone records. Some were spuriously questioned, so they could say they had done an investigation, but most were never questioned at all because they were too rich and powerful to be touched by the law.

It didn't matter. I knew the truth. And, so did Jack.

Time was running out. As absurd as the whole thing was, I had to find Count Malpheus. But, I had no idea how to go about it. Erika was unconscious most of the time, her phone had been stolen and her day planner was missing. There was not a trace of the man and all I knew about him was the name, "Count Malpheus."

In desperation, I placed a large classified ad in the newspaper, hoping he would see it. I could think of no other way.

"A Message to Count Malpheus: Someone dear to you is in trouble. To keep your promise, call 555-0198. Hurry! It is a matter of life and death."

The day after I ran that ad, I went to the hospital to see her, but she was not in her room. Frantic, I questioned the drone in white at the front desk and soon learned she was no longer at the hospital. She was at the city morgue!

I sat down and cried until I was sick. There was nothing else to do.

I went home in utter exhaustion and slept until nightfall. I took special care to lock my doors and took extra security precautions around the house as much as I could. I was afraid of Jack. I knew he killed Erika as surely as I knew my own name. And, I had ratted him out to the cops, although, it hadn't done any good.

I tried to sleep through the night, but failed. Maybe it was my fear of Jack or just the totality of what had so recently transpired. I cannot be sure. But, I didn't nod off until the sun came up the next morning.

When I finally woke up and was sipping my coffee while perusing the daily newspaper, I read the following headline: "Prostitute's Body Disappears from Morgue."

According to the brief article that followed, overnight the body of an unnamed prostitute disappeared without a trace from the premises, despite security. The article noted that details were limited due to an ongoing investigation into the subject's apparent murder.

My mind reeled with shock.

Her missing body added another dimension to the puzzle. It occurred to me that Jack might have tried to dispose of her body in order to avoid whatever evidence against him might turn up in the course of an autopsy. I tried to piece it all together, but I could not.

I don't remember much about the details of the next two or three days. I was emotionally devastated and had difficulty sleeping, especially at night.

The night Jack met his fate, I was home and wide awake. I can't tell you how nervous and anxious I was. It's difficult to describe the feeling of knowing something is wrong and yet not knowing exactly what it is. You try to talk yourself out of your fears, only to have them confirmed in some new, horrifying way.

I had locked myself inside my house for the past several days. I couldn't face the world or the people in it and the terrible things they were saying about Erika. They didn't know her like I did. They didn't know her intellect, her passions, her pain, her heart and her dreams. To them she was just a whore. And, that was reason enough to justify her murder in the eyes of more people than would admit it to you face to face.

I spent my time trying to distract myself. I caught up on novels and and watched movies, although, I struggled to maintain my focus on these things.

I remember lying on the sofa, with only the light of the television, finally reaching a very relaxed state when the phone rang. Startled, I sprang wide awake.

I had not answered the phone to anyone for days. But, this call seemed different. The caller I.D. was completely blank and it came at an unusual hour. I glanced at the time, it was around 3 a.m. I thought I should answer it.

"Hello"

"Hi! It's me."

It was Erika! "Where are you?" I asked, urgently.

"I'm with my husband, Count Malpheus," she said.

"Are you all right?"

"Yes," she said. "That's why I'm calling you. I wanted you to know that I'm fine."

"But, I thought you were dead. Weren't you at the morgue?"

"Yes, that's where he found me. I still had enough life force left in my body to be revivified. I'm immortal, now!" she laughed. "Please, tell everyone I'm all right."

"I will," I said.

"Oh! And, don't worry about Jack! He won't hurt you," she said.

"How do you know," I asked. I wanted to believe that, but I wasn't sure.

"He's dead! He was driving pretty fast on the freeway when he got a little fright," she laughed, again. But, this time there was hint of wickedness in it, as if she and the count had something to do with it. "He veered off the road and into some trees."

I was fine with that. "When will I see you, again?" I asked.

"I don't know," she said. "Maybe someday soon. You never know."

"No," I repeated, "You never know."

Her last words to me were, "I love you."

"I love you, too," I said. And, I hung up the phone, still uncertain whether I had dreamed the whole thing or not.

The next day, it was all over the news about Jack the guitarist wrapping his car around a tree. According to the official reports, the police theorized that he was frightened by the sudden appearance of something, maybe a large animal, in the middle of the highway and turned his steering wheel too sharply in an attempt to miss it, which caused him to lose control.

The wreck was spotted by a truck driver who reported it at about 2:45 a.m. According to the papers, Jack died instantly upon impact.

Now, you know the truth.

Sincerely,

A Friend of Erika

BLOOD AND STILETTOS: THE DIARY OF A VAMPIRE STRIPPER

DEDICATION

In loving memory of Anthony Vito, his son Raymond and all the other members of the Vampire Hunters Association who have given their lives in the quest for proof of the existence of vampires. You shall not be forgotten.

Sophia diGregorio

Blood and Stilettos

PROLOGUE

The following has been compiled from a series of journals and documents originally belonging to Matilda "Tilly" Rose Marlowe. They were discovered on October 13th, 2011 stored in a lead box, contained in the foundation of a house which was burned to the ground at the corner of Elm Street and Cedar Avenue in the City of Springfield. Excerpts are presented here in chronological order. The originals, which are in the possession of the National Vampire Hunters Association are available to researchers for examination by appointment only.

- National Vampire Hunters Association, Springfield Chapter
"We are dedicated to exposing the truth about vampires."

Sophia diGregorio

CHAPTER 1. MY EARLY LIFE

December 13, 1889

Today is my sixteenth birthday. I received several presents from my parents, among them a book, called "Laura Silver Bell," by Sheridan LeFanu, a monogrammed handkerchief embroidered by my mother and you, my dear diary.

I suppose I should begin writing by introducing myself to you. I was born on this date in 1873 in Hingham, Massachusetts. I am the only child of Joseph Marlowe and Lucinda Jane of the Gould family whose ancestors were among the earliest settlers here. I am named after my mother's mother, Matilda and my father's mother, Rose. But, my parents have always called me Tilly Rose.

My father is a merchant who has several stores in nearby towns, which stock the latest fur and shoe fashions. My parents have always been more than generous with me and I feel that I'm very fortunate compared to other girls my age. We live in the country and our life here is very simple. But, I've always had the finest clothes and novelties and I have never wanted for anything material or otherwise.

I have no brothers and sisters. My only other relatives are Aunt Josephine, Uncle Teddy and my cousins Eli, Jesse, Beth and Adeline who came to visit with my mother and me today because it was a special occasion. Although, I see them so rarely that they are almost like strangers to me.

It is rural and isolated where we live and there is an expanse of fields and farms that separates us from our neighbors. I spend most days studying for several hours. I have tutors for music, drawing and anything else my mother cannot teach me, herself. I think I'm best at dancing and drawing pictures. But, I can read and speak French and German very well.

Mother says I'm a loner because I prefer books to people and I don't really have any friends except my horse, Bonnie. I've always been very happy riding horses and reading books. Now that I have you, my dear diary, I feel I have a new friend. I don't have many secrets, but I promise to tell them all to you.

May 1, 1890

I attended my dear cousin Adeline's wedding to Cornelius Stratham. It was the most beautiful and romantic procession I have ever seen. I have never seen Adeline so beautiful, vibrant and happy as she was today clad in her green, satin dress with dogwood blossoms adorning her lovely hair.

As they exchanged their vows, she gazed into her new husband's eyes with unbound love and adoration. I fancied I could see angels plucking strains on their harps and singing above them as they formed their holy union.

I am sure that this auspicious day of new beginnings will prove a good omen for them.

Someday I will marry and I hope I shall be as happy as Adeline.

Mother took out the yolk of a boiled egg for me and filled it with salt. I will eat it tonight before I sleep so I will dream of my future husband!

July 4, 1890

My parents and I attended a Fourth of July celebration and barbecue where I was introduced to a very nice, young man named Phillip Ross. He is a distant cousin who recently lost his mother, so he has come to live with his uncle at a nearby farm.

He is a little too plain and simple to be the man of my dreams, but I find myself thinking about him constantly ever since this afternoon.

Is this love?

September 3, 1890

Tonight I attended a dance with my dearest Phillip. We have grown very close. I think he must be lonely because he has been visiting the house frequently ever since we met. It must be difficult for him in a new place, especially having so recently lost his mother.

We danced every dance together tonight. Even when another boy tried to cut in, he simply refused. I can't remember ever having more fun that I did tonight. I can't stop thinking about him.

October 28, 1890

I attended the annual country fair. Tonight Phillip and I held hands on a hay ride. He makes me laugh. How wonderful it is to be in love!

December 23, 1890

Cousin Adeline and her child are dead. She tripped on a loose piece of carpeting on the stairs and fell down the entire flight.

What a terrible blow to us all and at Christmas time, no less! How can there be happiness anywhere in the world when we are enduring such sorrow?

"Marry in the month of May and you'll surely rue the day." Poor Adeline!

December 26, 1890

The snow is knee deep and it is bitterly cold. We attended the funeral of Adeline and her baby. It will be days and perhaps weeks before they can receive a proper burial because the ground is frozen solid.

I heard something very disturbing at the funeral, something I almost cannot believe! But, I heard it with my own ears. Aunt Josephine whispered to Mother just loudly enough for me to hear her say that Cornelius never wanted children. My aunt suspects he only married Adeline to get his hands on her property. There is a rumor being whispered that Cornelius shoved her down the stairs. This is an unthinkable horror, yet I fear it might be true.

I shall never marry! I swear it before God and all the angels of Heaven!

February 14, 1891

Phillip has proposed. He actually fell upon one knee and presented me with a golden ring and asked, "Will you marry me?"

The words fell from his lips with such composed self-assurance, I'm certain he expected me to give my consent right away. I could not say the word, "No." In fact, I could not answer, at all. My throat became dry and tight and I seemed to choke on the very air. So, I said nothing. But, my answer was evident in my silence and he stormed out of the room in a rage.

While I enjoy spending time with him, the thought of marriage fills me with such apprehension that I feel ill. I have looked forward with dread to the day he might propose marriage to me ever since the tragic death of Adeline. I'm afraid this may mean the end of our friendship.

March 3, 1891

What a strange day this has been!

Phillip has announced his marriage to cousin Bernadette and the whole family is talking about it. This decision seems very hasty to me.

I fear I must have hurt Phillip very deeply with my refusal. But, I cannot help feeling relieved. I wish them well.

May 30, 1891

This evening we attended a small party at my aunt and uncle's house in celebration of cousins Eli and Jesse having graduated from medical school.

They both have promising futures ahead of them as successful medical doctors. I am very happy for them.

June 11, 1891

I attended Phillip and Bernadette's wedding. She wore a dark, red dress embellished with ribbons and bows.

She looked so beautiful!

I can't help thinking about the old saying, "Married in red, you'll wish yourself dead." But, that's just an old superstition.

January 11, 1892

Phillip is dead! He was riding his horse when it was suddenly spooked by something. It reared up several times, first throwing him to the ground then crashing down on his head with its hooves.

March 29, 1892

Bernadette's baby is born dead. The doctors say the shock of Phillip's death and her subsequent grief caused this to happen.

Poor Bernadette! Would this have been my fate had I married Phillip?

November 11, 1893

This afternoon, father was struck down by a runaway carriage.

Life seems to be full of endless sadness and pain. I fear nothing good will ever happen in my life, again. It seems as if the specter of death is looming over us all.

November 15, 1893

We attended father's funeral today.

His obituary:

A Tragic Death. Joseph Marlowe was hurled to Heaven after being struck by a runaway team of horses and a carriage owned by the Wynott Photography

Studio. According to witnesses, the horses took fright and nearly ran down several school children, who were unharmed before striking Mr. Marlowe as he was crossing Main Street at around 3 o'clock on Tuesday the 14th of November.

This day has been a complete blur. I am too upset to write more about this now.

August 3, 1894

There has been an inquest in which the deputy coroner ruled my father's death to be accidental. Mother is to receive a fairly large death settlement.

Words cannot describe what a painful loss we have suffered!

November 1, 1894

Mother is dead. Her heart simply stopped. I believe she died of grief.

Whatever will become of me? I am completely alone in the world. I don't know what to do!

November 5, 1894

Mother's obituary:

Last Monday Mrs. Lucinda Jane Marlowe, widow of Mr. Joseph Marlowe, died suddenly after retiring to bed at her usual hour. At around 5 o' clock in the morning, her daughter was aroused from sleep by a clatter from the bedroom. She found her mother lying on the floor, the spark of life flown from her eyes. The doctor was called, but it was too late. He later named the cause of death as neuralgia of the heart.

Mrs. Marlowe was the daughter of Mr. Arthur Gould and was 54-years old. A brother, a sister and a daughter mourn their loss. Funeral services will take place today at the Old Church at 4 o' clock.

December 3, 1894

I have inherited a modest amount of property and wealth and I am free of financial worries. Yet, I gaze upon the future with fear. I know not why.

Every day is cold and gray and I am tormented by pangs of emptiness.

April 23, 1894

I have endured an insufferable barrage of visits from gentlemen callers since the snow has cleared. I do not care for their company. They frighten me as I am here all alone. Fortunately, father showed me how to handle a shotgun and shoot straight!

January 5, 1895

The stock market has taken a few too many sour turns. Many of my father's investments have become worthless. Fortunately, I still have this property and a few other assets to sustain me.

I'm sure this will all turn around soon and my luck will improve.

December 13, 1897

The economic crisis has finally reached my front door. Father's investments in the railroads and other unfortunate stocks along with the onslaught of banking and credit fraud have led to the depletion of my fortune.

Barring a miracle, I fear I will be out of money in a few months.

July 8, 1898

What am I going to do? I cannot describe the panic that grips my heart at this moment. I can no longer afford to pay upkeep on the house or taxes. I can barely manage to keep food in my mouth.

Maybe I should have married. But, I probably would have ended up like Adeline or Bernadette! Besides, now that I have no more money, I have no more suitors. There is no work for me here except for taking in neighbors' clothes to wash and mend. If I stay, I will surely die of hunger. But, I have nowhere to go.

I must think about what to do. If only I could ask Father or Mother!

August 1, 1898

"The desperate disease requires a dangerous remedy," as someone once said. I have taken an apartment in an inexpensive, but disreputable part of the City and I found a job working for a milliner. I was hired by Horace Washington and his son Herbert who is the overseer of production at the Washington Hat Co.

August 3, 1898

My world is now one of tulle, straw, felt, velvet, silk, ribbons and plumes. The millinery is hot and miserable. We must meet quotas and Herbert is a cruel slave driver. I despise him!

August 15, 1898

Will this suffocating heat never end? It is miserably hot in the factory. My fingers are so sore with cuts and bruises from hat-making that I can barely hold a pen.

I had an unpleasant encounter with Herbert today. He does not seem pleased with my work, although it is better than that of most of the other girls. Something about him repulses me. I cannot explain it. I would like to find another job, but I don't know how I can! I can't afford to miss a day's work, as it is.

October 22, 1898

I am shaking with fear as I write this, but I must write because I have no one else to tell. One of the girls I work with has disappeared without a trace.

She is the fourth woman to disappear in the past few weeks. The other three were found strangled with a red cloth. All of them worked in the same industrial area of town where I work.

October 25, 1898

An iceman making early deliveries found my colleague's body floating in a ravine not far from her apartment. Like the others, she had a red cloth wrapped around her throat.

The police do not have any leads. Despite posturing by the chief of police in the newspaper, it doesn't appear that they're trying very hard to find the killer.

November 3, 1898

Another woman from a nearby garment factory has been strangled to death. Her body was found in a trash dumpster only a few blocks from the millinery. This is the fifth murder!

It's all very disconcerting. I hope the police catch the killer soon.

November 16, 1898

Everyone is very frightened as another one of our colleagues has gone missing. She and I are friends, although I don't really know her outside of work. She is a very sweet, strawberry blonde, freckle-faced girl who never has an unkind word to say about anyone.

We have all been advised to stay together when we leave work and not go out after dark. But, this is useless advice as it is impossible for all of us to go everywhere in the company of another person. There is always a time when I am alone going to and from work or other places I have to go.

Oh, why can't the police catch the killer of so many women?

Sophia diGregorio

CHAPTER 2. MY NEW LIFE

November 21, 1898

Have I succumbed to madness? My mind cannot conceive of such horrors as have taken place over the past couple of days. I feel as if the entire world has been pulled out from under my feet like a rug. I cannot believe that what I'm about to describe is real or even possible.

My mind is still reeling from this bizarre series of events. Nonetheless, I shall try to relate what has happened, giving every detail I can remember.

It was Friday, just three nights ago, when Herbert kept me after work to correct a large number of hats he said were improperly constructed. In fact, the hats were fine; it was all a charade. But, I went through the motions of taking them apart and fixing them while he supervised.

He said that if I didn't start doing a better job, he would have to let me go, unless I would be interested in an arrangement where I would perform certain personal services for him. I did not respond to these advances. He grabbed me by the shoulders and said, "I can destroy you! Do you understand?"

I looked him straight in the eyes and told him that if he didn't take his hands off me he would regret it. His eyes appeared to go black as his face contorted with rage, but he had no other response to this. Then, he let me go and stormed out of the room.

I was left alone because all of the other girls had already gone home. I had to walk up the darkened sidewalk at night by myself. It was there, just steps away from the entry to my apartment building that I was yanked off my feet. A man grabbed me by my ankles and dragged me down the alley behind some debris.

I screamed for help in those moments, but if anyone heard, no one came. He launched the most vicious assault on my person before strangling me with a cloth he pulled from his pocket and leaving me to die in a pool of my own blood.

I do not know how long I lay there. I faded in and out of consciousness. My only thought was of the great pain I was in. I could think of nothing else, nor could I feel any emotion. There was only pain and a sense of my life force ebbing. I knew I was dying, but that was all I knew. I did not have the energy or force of mind to think or reason.

As the night grew blacker, I became aware of a shadowy figure emerging from the darkness. I was frightened because I thought surely it was the man who attacked me, returning to make sure I was dead. But, I was too weak to stir as much as a finger.

I sensed the nearby presence of a man, but not the one who had previously attacked me. I was aware that he knelt by my side and took my wrist. I felt a sharp pain as he sank his teeth into my flesh and I heard the sounds of a wildly feeding animal as he sucked the last drop of blood from my veins.

I was dead. I know this with certainty. I died in that moment, I was aware of nothing but a painful silence. The terrible events of the past several years of my life, all of the deaths and torment assailed my mind in one horrifying moment and then there was nothing more.

In that one moment, the Hell of the life I had known ended.

I remained in silent darkness, aware of nothing, until I awoke in a different place. I found myself in a dark, windowless room, my mind in a state of muddled confusion. The atmosphere was musty and stale and the sounds of dripping water echoing throughout the chamber enhanced the chilling dampness that permeated the air.

I heard a faint rustling sound, possibly the scurrying of rats, I thought. I tried to make sense of what had just happened, but I could not.

It seemed an interminable length of time passed. Then, I heard the faint sound of footsteps approaching, followed by the sound of a door creaking on its hinges as someone entered the room.

I was not afraid. The terrifying ordeal I had just suffered seemed to have rendered me incapable of feeling fear or any other emotion. Yet, my vision seemed to have grown keener, for even as I remained lying still in the darkness, I could make out the outline of a tall figure wearing a stovepipe hat and a full cape.

After a moment, I heard the sound of a match being struck and saw the flame of an oil lamp as it was lit across the room. The sound of footsteps drew closer, bearing with them the dimly glowing light.

For the first time, I saw the face of my savior, somewhat long and gaunt with sharp features, full sensual lips and dark eyes. He removed his hat as he sat down beside where I lay outstretched on a sofa. His hair was shoulder length, pitch black and straight. Although, pale and vaguely cadaverous, he was handsome.

He stretched out his long, pale hand and touched my shoulder.

"Where am I?" I asked. My own voice sounded strange and far away to me, as if it came from the depths of a well.

"You are safe here with me in the bowels of the city."

"Who are you?"

"Vasco Valverde," he said. "I'm sure you feel a little strange right now, but in a very short time, you will be fine. In fact, you will feel better than you've ever felt in your life."

"What happened to me? Do you know?" I asked. The memories were foggy at this point, but they were coming back to me in bits and snatches.

"I found you in an alley on the verge of death and I brought you here."

"Yes," I said. "I remember you doing something. What was it?" In a moment, I could almost see the scene as if I were hovering above my own body. "Yes. You sucked the blood from my wrist. Why did you do that?"

"It was all I could do," he said. "Otherwise, you would not be here. You would have eventually been found dead like the other women."

"The other women," I repeated as memories flooded into my mind. "I remember. Yes!" I could remember the smell of my attacker as if it were still in my nostrils. I knew with certainty that the man in my presence was not him. "There is a killer of women loose on the streets, one the police cannot seem to catch!" I said. I sat up in a panic as I now recalled the killer's scent with the most vivid realism. "And, I know who he is! I must go to the police at once. It is my duty!"

"Wait a moment," he said. "Think! Is there a better way? The police can't catch a killer. What does this mean?"

"I don't know," I said. "I've been asking myself why they couldn't stop these crimes. I don't have an answer."

"It's not their primary business to catch killers," he said, smiling grimly. "They derive no direct benefit from either preventing or prosecuting such crimes and neither does the city they work for. So, this is a murderer's paradise."

"I don't understand," I said, dumbfounded. "What is your point?"

"If they can't catch him, then they can't catch us, either."

"What are you suggesting?"

"Dinner!" he said, licking his lips.

I was puzzled by this, but I would not remain so for long as he explained to me in detail the circumstances of my having been reborn that night as a vampire.

The very word, "vampire," appears ludicrous to me, even now as I write it. Yet, I cannot deny my own experience, this inexplicable sense of calm and the peculiar thirst for human blood.

Every muscle in my body seems filled with an exhilarating, inhuman strength and power. I feel invincible, as if I could leap mountains. And, I find I have new passions unlike any I have known before.

On the night I died and was resurrected, I was reborn to a new life. Now, I stand on the precipice of a bold, new future, which I hope will finally be free of misery and fear.

November 23, 1898

I find myself overcome by the strangest desires. Vasco and I were lying together here in this dark, underground chamber beneath the city sidewalks and while I gazed upon his face, I found myself longing to be touched in ways I never imagined before.

Is this some strange power he has over me? Or, is it a power of my own and part of this new life? Which it is, I cannot tell for certain, but, it is overwhelming.

As we lay wrapped in each other's arms, he told me the story of how he came to be a vampire. His parents arrived in Mexico in 1780 and both his father and grandfather fought in the Mexican War of Independence against Spain. He was only a child when it first began. But, as he grew older, this ideal of freedom, latent in his veins was roused and he, too, took up arms against the invaders and their royalist supporters.

He survived the war and would have been happy to return to living on the outskirts of a quiet town with his horses and cattle, but this was not to be. Upon returning home, he found his ranch had been burned to the ground, all of his livestock were gone and most of his family had been murdered by marauders.

With no home left, he wandered northward, crossed the gulf and arrived in Louisiana where he stayed for a short time. There, in New Orleans, he became a professional gambler. By virtue of his uncanny ability to calculate the cards in his opponents' hands, he soon became a gentleman in possession of a small fortune. He lived in the best hotels, drank in the best saloons and generally led the life of a young libertine in a city characterized by all manner of vices.

Ironically, his good fortune at gambling was the cause of his undoing. He was playing especially well one night and had amassed quite a sum by the time the final game was over. Upon returning to his hotel, he was approached by two men who gunned him down in the street, took his money and ran away in the early hours of the morning, while most of the city still lay sleeping.

He was found a short time later by a vampire who bestowed a new life upon him, just as the last breath would have escaped his body. The vampire's legacy was the salvation of dying innocents. This was where Vasco learned to give life to others in the throes of death.

Once he became comfortable with his new life, he grew restless and traveled around the states and territories until arriving in New England, where he has remained ever since, finding the climate more compatible with his constitution.

I was moved by this story. As he told it, I gazed upon his face and watched the pain of these memories play out in the sadness of his eyes. I know what it is to lose everything and have nowhere to go. And, I was filled with gratitude to him for having rescued me from the clutches of a very final death.

With these thoughts, I found myself overcome with a desire I have never felt for any man before, not even Phillip, who now seems a distant memory, like a dream.

As if pulled by some magnetic force, our lips met. Our kisses were tenuous, at first, and filled with some sense of timid uncertainty. Soon, they became more intense and passionate until I was conscious of nothing else.

After some time, I was overcome by a primal desire to feel his bare skin against my own. Instinctively, I began unbuttoning his shirt. He gave no resistance. Once I had removed this garment, he methodically removed my blouse and undergarments.

The friction of our bodies produced a sense of profound satisfaction in me, as if a great, long-standing yearning had been satisfied. Yet, in a short time, it seemed as if this was not enough. I wanted more.

With a hunger driven by passion the likes of which I have never know before, I longed to feel even closer to him. Involuntarily, my hands were drawn to the fastener of his trousers and in a matter of moments, I had removed the last fiber of clothing and any barrier of my own which had been between us.

His strong, slender body moved against mine in a natural rhythm as we continued to kiss, entwined in each other's arms. His hands moved gently and my body ached with the sweetest desire. Just when I could tolerate this agonizing state of excitement not a second longer, he did what we both longed to do.

His motions were steady and gentle and I was glad to be in the hands of such an experienced and spirited lover. Gasping and moaning with heretofore unknown pleasure, I was seized by a series of spasms and sense of warmth flooding throughout my body. Vasco increased the rhythm of his motions culminating in convulsions of pleasure, which gave me an inexplicable delight to see and feel.

We enjoyed these rapturous sensations together, while wrapped in each others arms.

Now, after such unspeakable tragedy, I find that I am free from misery and fear and living a life of the greatest satisfaction. I want for nothing and I can breathe freely. For the first time in my life, I feel liberated and alive.

My memory is strong and so are my senses. I know who attacked me and who still lurks in the alleys at night waiting to prey upon innocents. I am no longer able to work at the millinery, but I have not forgotten my colleagues. I cannot forget them nor can I forget the danger in which they all remain.

Yet, tonight my thoughts are dominated by more pleasant matters. I am in love with the vampire Vasco Valverde.

November 27, 1898

This evening, we hunted for my killer. I was certain that the perpetrator was none other than Herbert, my former boss. I remembered that Herbert often enjoys a few drinks at a tavern called The Pink Poodle in the evening. We went to see if he was there.

I was astounded to see him sitting there at the bar. I recognized his scent even before he came into view. The blood of evil people has a spicy aroma and a murderer's scent is as unique as a signature.

We sat down, ordered a drink and waited. I could see his face reflected in the mirror behind the bar. At one point he saw me, too - the person he murdered! His face turned ashen white with horror. As if paralyzed by fear, he sat at the bar, downing one drink after another and furtively glancing at me in the mirror, until closing time. By that time, he was very unsteady on his feet.

We were right behind him when he left the bar. We followed him for some distance. All the while, he was well aware that he was being followed. He turned around a few times to toss us a look of absolute terror, then stumbled along faster down the sidewalk.

When we reached a place of complete darkness, where the shadows obscured all, I seized the fiend by the neck from behind and dragged him with all of my newly found strength into a nearby alley. There, under Vasco's watchful eye, I sucked his blood down to very nearly the last drop.

Vasco instructed me how to carefully drain the blood of our prey without creating another like ourselves. The last few drops of blood must be preserved, then the subject is killed by some other means. I learned the secret to either bestowing immortality or causing permanent death.

After I satisfied my thirst, I broke his neck under Vasco's approving eye and we took his body to the river, dropped it in and watched it sink under the waves.

It took all my will power to comply when Vasco told me to stop drinking this red, liquid life force. I can still taste his blood in my mouth. There is no finer cuisine!

No delicacy of the human palate can compare or impart such energy and strength.

Tonight is a triumph. The predator became prey!

The thrill of the kill is an unexpected aphrodisiac. The effects are dizzying. Vasco and I made the most passionate love afterward. We could hardly wait to be alone again.

Breathing hard, we crossed the threshold of our lair, hastily shed our clothes and embraced as if we would never let go of each other, seemingly mingling our essences, even our very souls. It's as if a bond between us has been sealed by this night's events.

December 18, 1898

I am enjoying my new found sense of freedom and my love affair with Vasco Valverde. I can remember no greater time in my life than now. I have never felt such devotion to another, nor can I recall experiencing such a sense of belonging since I lost my family, which seems so long ago.

I believe there is nothing in the world more important than passion. There is no real living without it. To be without it, even for mortals, represents a living death.

Vasco and I live by night. As twilight descends every evening, we make love. We roam the city streets, the country roads, cemeteries and all of the places mere mortals fear to tread after dark. Sometimes we feed upon the miscreants we find. Con artists have their own special flavor as do thieves and sexual deviants. The area close to the river is a veritable smorgasbord of culinary temptations.

Occasionally, Vasco goes to a gambling hall and I go out on my own to theaters and musical performances.

April 23, 1899

Life is good. I hope things stay this way forever!

December 18, 1899

Something strange is happening. We are being pursued by a group of men. We do not know why, but they have dogged our every step for the past several days. Who are they and what do they want?

December 23, 1899

I am very worried. Vasco has not returned. He went to one of his favorite gambling houses and vanished. I do not know where he is, but I sense he has not gone far. I will wait.

February 11, 1900

I am unbearably alone. I have searched everywhere for Vasco. I have sought him in every gambling house in the city and at all our usual haunts, but there is no sign of him.

March 3, 1901

I have come to terms with my solitude.

I kill to live on in strength until the time I am reunited with Vasco. My appetite is strong. I never slay innocents, but seek the evil-doers in the night. Their blood is sweetest upon my lips.

I sleep at the cemetery in a family mausoleum. No one disturbs me here. At sundown, I prowl the city. I am Queen of the Night. But, it is a lonely reign.

I continue to search for Vasco.

June 14, 1906

I am sad and alone in the world. I have sought Vasco in every nighttime establishment in the city to no avail. I am in despair. I cannot go on like this any longer. I will sleep.

April 6, 1917

I awoke at nightfall. There is strange, sad silence in the air.

A newspaper was blowing along the city street. I picked it up and read the date. I was shocked to see that I had slept for so many years. Then, I noticed the headline: "U.S. Declares War on Germany."

It seems things have not improved. But, I have only two thoughts: Blood and Vasco.

I browsed the obituaries and articles on crimes trying to find a clue to Vasco's whereabouts, but I found nothing of interest there. I looked for him up and down every street and alley in this part of the city. But, I did not find him.

Finally, I dined on a Mafioso dressed in a fur coat and a plumed, felt hat outside a night club. I can taste his evil deeds in his blood. This one was particularly satisfying. Now, his remains are food for the river fish.

April 30, 1917

I have looked for Vasco every night from dusk until dawn. There's not a trace of him, yet I sense he is nearby.

Tonight I came across an office building bearing the name, "The Vampire Hunters Association." Maybe I am not the only one looking for Vasco. I plan to investigate further, but with discretion. These people sound like they could be dangerous.

May 1, 1917

I slipped into the Vampire Hunters' headquarters late tonight and looked at their documents. They have no information about Vasco, only a list of other suspected vampires.

Most of them are people who have gone missing, are victims of crimes or are criminals themselves. The list includes one of my former co-workers from the millinery. Most, if not all, of the names listed are innocent. What fools these men are! How could such idiots possibly be dangerous to anyone?

Once again, I feel alone and disappointed. If the Vampire Hunters Association had turned out to be authentic, I might have found a clue to Vasco's whereabouts. Or, I might have found others like myself.

June 6, 1917

The most remarkable thing happened earlier tonight. I followed a couple through an alley, into the back door of Fiorelli's Burlesque Theater. I thought one of the couple was Vasco, but after I had a closer look, I saw that I was mistaken. I found myself in the backstage area. I was mistaken for a performer, assailed by a make-up artist, hurried into a sequined corset and fishnet stockings and hustled onto the stage.

At first, I was a little uncertain about what to do, but I just followed the music, kept smiling and added a touch of humor. The crowd went wild with applause at the end. It was such a wonderful feeling!

The theater manager realized his mistake, but since the audience liked my performance, he hired me on the spot.

Sophia diGregorio

CHAPTER 3. MY LIFE OF BURLESQUE

June 8, 1917

This was my first real night as an entertainer. Backstage isn't nearly as glamorous as the stage, itself. But, Mr. Fiorelli who owns the theater is very fatherly and kind. Each person here, including the management, the musicians, comedians and actors, possesses a unique personality.

The pay is not great, but I enjoy the applause and the company of the other dancers who are the kindest, most candid and energetic people I've ever met. I feel right at home.

I love the costumes and the make-up. It's a funny thing about make-up; it can hide what you are while making you appear as you are not. No one suspects that I'm a vampire.

Most of all, I love my new entertainment family. We sleep all day and come alive at night. We live our lives with zest and moxie.

It eases the pain of losing Vasco, although I still find myself searching the audience for him every night.

June 20, 1917

I have never met more wonderful women than those of the burlesque stage. Sometimes we go out after Fiorelli's closes. The dancers have a refreshingly frank, open way of speaking and I enjoy these hours discussing the intimate details of their lives over coffee and pie in late night delicatessens.

December 31, 1917

I have saved enough money to move out of the cemetery. I almost feel like an ordinary human being, again.

April 20, 1923

Six years of relative peace and tranquility were dashed to pieces tonight!

I'm still bewildered at all that has happened.

Tonight as La Bella Donna gave her performance at the center stage along with a couple of the other girls, they noticed the appearance of police lining the back wall of the theater. Naturally, they found this disconcerting. But, like true professionals, they finished their act without missing a beat. As they received their applause and exited the stage, the cops suddenly rushed into the backstage and dressing room area.

Men in the dressing room! It's so shocking. This is never permitted.

Most of my colleagues, in fact, all of the women, were hunted down like animals by these huge armed men. This is one of the most singularly terrifying moments of my life. Yet, I escaped.

It happened like in a dream, where you can change forms and places instantly. In this moment of terror, I transformed myself and escaped by perching on a rafter high above. I could feel that I was in a different body, a small, inhuman one. It seems to me that it happened instinctively and I'm not sure I could consciously repeat it. Until tonight, I did not know I had this ability.

From my perch above, I witnessed numerous abuses of my colleagues by police as they literally chased them throughout the theater, dashed them to the floor and molested them.

Despite the fact that there is a rash of seemingly unrelated violent crimes in the area, the police came into the theater and attacked innocent women in this cowardly fashion. How can this be? The police are supposed to fight crimes, not commit them.

Why would they waste their time here, when there is a rash of nighttime violence in this area? I cannot make sense of it.

I am very sad and frightened because of this police raid, which must surely be illegal. It is an unprovoked, unwarranted attack on the only family I have!

April 24, 1923

It is worse than I thought! In the dressing room tonight, one of my colleagues told me she was intimately attacked by a police sergeant named Bartholomew, while she was being held at the jail. Overhearing this, a second girl told of being violently groped by another uniformed thug named Pullman.

The charges against the theater are vague, but center on accusations of obscenities and lewdness, which are patently false. We still do not know the real motivation for this attack by the police.

Sophia diGregorio

The show goes on, but the anger and trepidation are palpable. Our sense of safety is shattered. It feels as if a dark cloud hangs over us.

April 30, 1923

It's my night off. It's nice to have an evening away from work. I usually enjoy the theater, but now everything has seemed so strained and a deep sadness lingers in the air, no matter how hard we try to maintain our levity.

I decided to make good use of my time. I already had a good description of Sgt. Bartholomew from the dancers, so I waited for a large, fat man with a bulbous nose to emerge from the back door of the police station at shift change.

While I waited, I thought about what it would take to bring happiness back to the theater again and restore our sense of safety and justice. I could only think of one solution. The perpetrators of these heinous crimes against us all must be eliminated. I considered the methods I might use, although I knew it would likely be a matter of opportunity, it was clear to me that it must appear to be an accident or suicide.

Suddenly, I spotted him. He left the precinct and walked to a local tavern where he remained long enough to guzzle down a couple of shots of whiskey. Then, he hailed a cab. I hailed another right behind him and followed him to an apartment building in a tidy, modestly prosperous-looking part of town.

Of course, he was a little tipsy and it was late at night, but he did not notice that he was being tailed. I wonder if many people in the city enter their apartments late at night with such a sense of safety and security. Possibly this is the singular privilege of a lawman, which other people in the city, particularly women, are not afforded.

Blood and Stilettos

Without once looking over his shoulder, he confidently climbed the stairs to the fourth floor, approached the door of his apartment, fumbled for his keys and, finally, opened the door and stepped inside. He would have closed the door behind him, but I prevented him from doing so. In an instant, I was in the room with him and we were alone.

His first cowardly impulse was to pull out his gun and point it at my face. When I laughed at him, he looked dismayed and withdrew it. "Who are you? What are you doing here?" he demanded. There was a well-practiced ring of confidence in his voice, but I could see he was afraid.

"I'm a citizen and I'm here in search of justice, Sgt. Bartholomew. You are Sgt. Bartholomew, aren't you?"

"I am."

"Why did your men conduct a raid on Fiorelli's?"

"We do what the mayor says," he said.

"You just blindly follow orders, even illegal ones, without ever asking questions?"

"I'm just doing my job," he said.

"But, why Fiorelli's? No laws were being broken. Tell me the real reason. I know you know!"

"Mr. Fiorelli should be more careful when he makes campaign contributions," Sgt. Bartholomew intimated.

"Elaborate!" I commanded.

"He contributed to the mayor's competitor in the last election, so we're making sure he knows not to do that, again. That's all."

"And, what about the innocent people you've arrested? What about the misery you've caused?"

"What's the big deal?" he shrugged. These were the words of a man without a soul.

"And, your disgusting treatment of my colleague?" I asked. "What do you have to say about that?"

"It was just a little sex. She enjoyed it. She's a dancer!

So what?"

Clearly, there was no point in further conversation. I had my answer regarding the motives for the raid. I followed my impulse and knocked the insolent swine out with one swift blow to the head. He fell over with a heavy thud.

The blood of sexual deviants has a particularly pungent scent and spicy flavor, something like curry and hot peppers. I drained his blood with relish, taking care not to leave a drop on the floor and holding back my appetite, so as not to draw the very last of his life force. This procedure rendered his corpulent carcass somewhat lighter than before.

By this time, it was very late at night, in fact, it was well past two o'clock and there was little traffic. I considered the possibility of taking the body to the river, but it didn't seem practical. Then, I remembered having passed a construction site some two or three blocks before arriving at the apartment.

I am especially strong right after feeding. Furthermore, my strength was fueled by my rage at this degenerate, whose nearly bloodless corpse now lay at my feet. I scooped up his remains and hauled them over my shoulder to the site. Using the shovels and tools at my disposal, I buried him there. His body will soon be covered by the foundation of a large building. The ground there is already disturbed, so no one will think anything about it. They'll never look for him there!

The world already seems to be a happier place now that one more evil soul has been laid to rest. With no body, there is no evidence of a crime having been committed. His disappearance will remain an unsolved mystery.

I only regret that I must celebrate this small triumph alone. How I miss Vasco!

May 4, 1923

A few days have passed since my encounter with Sgt. Bartholomew and I've since spoken to Mr. Fiorelli. He suspects political motivations for the attacks on the club, but he is not certain of it. Of course, I am certain. But, I cannot tell him how I know.

Officer Pullman who was named as a groper by more than one of my colleagues met an untimely death earlier this night. I planned this venture more carefully than the last. Having so recently dined, I was better able to control my appetite.

As has become common in the city, yet another murderer is on the loose. He has left a string of unsolved murders behind him and the police won't catch him because, as Vasco once said, it's not their real business.

The death of Officer Pullman will appear as only another of these murders to them, if they ever locate his body, which they won't. I buried it, with the utmost care, in a wooded area near the river.

September 28, 1923

The latest news, which has everyone worried, concerns the intensification of violent crime in the city. It's another day and yet another young working class woman is dead.

Do policemen have souls? Given their conduct toward us, I do not believe they have any intention of ever solving these crimes, despite increased public pressure, as there are too many rogue elements within the department. It is reminiscent of the series of unsolved murders surrounding the factory district, which led to my own death.

Although, the women at the theater are concerned about the killer who has not yet been caught, the biggest predators we have to worry about are the police, themselves. It is the most immediate threat. We live in constant fear of yet another violent police raid on the club, which is far greater than the fear of being murdered because while the former is imminent, the latter is a matter of chance and might be avoidable. This anxiety mars every minute of our lives at the theater, whether we're on the stage or in the dressing room.

October 24, 1923

I don't know why I didn't think of it before! Of course, it is a desperate outside shot, but I have an idea about how to contact my lost love.

I rented a private mailbox and placed a classified ad asking for Vasco to send a letter to Tilly. Unfortunately, I've checked the mail box the last three days and found nothing.

October 31, 1923

I am elated! Today I received the following correspondence:

Dearest Tilly,

Meet me at the Mercury Cafe at 11 p.m. on Saturday.

With All My Love,

V.V.

November 3, 1923

It has been an enlightening and eventful evening, although, not what I expected.

Blood and Stilettos

I kept my appointment to meet Vasco, arriving a few minutes early. As I approached the Mercury Cafe, I was ambushed by five men wielding torches and knives.

Despite the fact that they were well-armed and I was outnumbered, I fought them off, snarling and hissing at them. The cowards turned and fled in terror.

I'm trying to sort out what happened.

Now, that I have had time to think about it, I am left to deduce that they were the true authors of the letter from Vasco. Furthermore, I am certain I recognized one of the villains as a member of the gang of police who raided us.

Could it be that Vasco is, in fact, nearby and that someone else is looking for him? It seems likely to me that the perpetrators are vampire hunters. If so, maybe they have more information.

I believe I will make a search of their headquarters, again. Maybe they actually know the whereabouts of other vampires in the city. One thing is certain, I won't run any more classified advertisements.

November 6, 1923

Once again, we were the subject of a particularly lewd and violent raid by the local police department. Mr. Fiorelli says it will be the last such incident because he has decided to close the theater and take the show on the road.

After a little consideration, I have decided not to go, although I have the sense that a noose is tightening around all our throats. The oppression is palpable. I am very saddened by this assault on our most basic liberties. Where will these injustices lead?

I feel that Vasco is nearby. I feel it so strongly! I cannot let go of the idea of seeing him, again.

Now, I am feeling very melancholy. There is nothing

Sophia diGregorio

left for me in this world. I am exhausted and I want to sleep. I will stay at the cemetery tonight. Here I will find peace.

CHAPTER 4. MY LIFE AS A GO-GO DANCER

March 16, 1965

Tonight, I awoke to thunderous noises, which shook the very earth. I left my repose to discover the source of the terrible noise and as the sounds grew louder I could see the construction of a very large, new road underway. Bright lights shone down as large equipment dug into the earth.

The atmosphere feels light and there is something reassuring in the night air. There is a sense of joy, even on this cloudy night. I feel as if I have been a prisoner and the doors have just opened. I do not know the cause of this sensation.

I toured downtown on foot, peering into the windows of the shops and looking at the cars and people. What has been decades seems like only yesterday. How the world has changed!

I must find new clothes. Mine are terribly out of vogue.

August 12, 1965

I auditioned at a night club called Club Royale and was hired as a dancer. It's much like the burlesque theater, but they call it "go-go dancing" and there are no elaborate acts or comedians, just dancers. The pay is much better. More importantly, I have a family, once again.

October 14, 1965

I love the new music, the clothes and the dance styles. So much has changed, but the girls of the stage remain the same kindly, rugged individualists. I enjoy their company at work and occasionally after hours. They are wonderfully open and talk very freely about their sexual adventures and many boyfriends.

I feel very good about this life. Although, I often think of Vasco and I miss him desperately. There are so many young, pretty, long-haired boys, especially at the after hours clubs. I admire them, but I am never tempted. I can think of no one else besides Vasco.

December 29, 1965

Tonight I saw "Doctor Zhivago." What a remarkable thing the cinema is! I missed so many things during my long sleep.

January 5, 1966

Tonight something a little disturbing happened. For some unknown reason, police squad cars sat on our parking lot all night, frightening away most of the patrons. The cops never came inside, though.

The club owner called it harassment. The dancers are whispering that it happened because of his refusal to give into demands for shakedown payments from the police.

That old feeling of foreboding has returned to me. It's as if some dark, nebulous cloud looms over the club, now.

January 7, 1966

They say that history repeats itself, but this is not really true. It is all a continuum, with the same actors with almost the same faces, committing the same acts, again and again.

Predictably, the club was raided tonight. This time the police were more violent than before. I watched as huge, armed men lasciviously assaulted the dancers who were in various stages of undress in the sanctity of our dressing room.

From the rafters above, I saw them wrestle petite women, tottering on high-heels to the cement floor in the most lewd and brutal way. It is a terrible thing to see, especially when I am helpless to do anything for them in the moment.

The entertainers were all charged as prostitutes. This is an outrage!

January 14, 1966

Whatever their political motives, the personal motives of the police always seem to remain the same. One of my colleagues was strangled and brutally assaulted by a policeman named Pillsbury while in custody. She has a lot of bruises and pain. Although, it doesn't appear, at this time, that there was any permanent injury, she is severely shaken by the attack.

She says Pillsbury spoke to her very disrespectfully, using street slang she couldn't understand. Suddenly, he became insanely angry, lunged at her and seized her by the throat. He strangled her just enough so she couldn't fight back, while he sexually attacked her. Of course, there are no witnesses and she knows no one will believe her because no one wants to believe the police are doing these things.

I believe her because I have seen how the police behave. I know their character because I can smell it in their blood. Only now, it seems even worse than before.

February 12, 1966

Officer Pillsbury has met an untimely death. Presently, what is left of his body is making its way out to sea. The blood of the wicked still has its same delightful flavor.

I lingered for some time by the river tonight taking in the cold night air as it wafted off the water. It's exhilarating. And, for some reason, it gives me a sense of hope.

March 2, 1966

I overheard a conversation tonight between two dancers about an illegal gambling house called the Tiger's Club. They said a lot of wealthy men go there on the weekends. This sounds like the kind of place Vasco might go.

It's a long shot, but I plan to investigate.

March 3, 1966

I followed this new lead directly to the back door of a private club. I could hardly believe my eyes when I saw Vasco, who seems completely unchanged. He was clad in a black suit with a red tie and sitting in the corner of the smoke-filled room, concentrating very deeply on his game.

I walked over to where he was seated and stood where he could get a clear view of me. It was a short time before he looked up from his cards. When he did, a big smile came across his face, he folded his hand and we walked outside together to talk.

"Where have you been?" I asked. "I've been looking for you for years!"

"The night I didn't come home, I left the gambling hall and was attacked by a group of men who called themselves vampire hunters. I transformed myself to elude them and in the course flight, I became trapped in a small chamber in an old, crumbling building. I was finally released when it was demolished just a few days ago," he explained.

He asked me where I had been for these past years. I explained that I was working as a dancer at the Club Royale and that we had been having a lot of problems with predatory police.

Coincidentally, as I was explaining all of this, we saw a couple of men leaving the gambling hall and I recognized them as raiding police officers. The aroma of their corrupt blood curling in my nostrils confirmed this fact.

We followed them a short distance. When the moment seemed right, we each seized one of the men from behind and drank their blood to the penultimate drop. After we feasted on the two rogues, we broke their pathetic necks and hastily tossed their bodies into a nearby trash dumpster.

Vasco and I have taken up right where we left off. We retired to one of my favorite mausoleums and made the most desperate love to each other there in the damp, dark chill. His skin is still as white as marble. His face is the most beautiful I've ever seen. As we kissed, tears rolling down our cheeks, I wondered if this was even real - after so long!

The feel of his breath upon my skin still transports me. The very touch of his slender hands upon my hand has the power to entrance me. He kissed me with those full, sensual lips in the same old gentle way. No sooner did he touch his lips to my most intimate regions, did I find my entire body awash in heat. The pulsations came quickly and I was overcome. Again and again, lost in this embrace, we crested and fell together like the waves of an ocean.

I vow never to know the pain of losing him, again!

March 5, 1966

Perhaps we were too indiscreet with the corpses of those two police officers.

This Saturday afternoon, as we slept in peaceful repose in our sanctuary in the cemetery, we were surrounded by men bearing torches and screaming threats at us.

They were soon driven off by the cemetery's caretaker. We are quite certain the perpetrators are from the Vampire Hunters Association. They have already caused us a lot of grief.

We are moving tonight!

March 6, 1966

We have taken up new lodgings in the cellar of a long-abandoned house. We are still discussing our options with regard to the vampire hunters. We know we must eliminate them, however, we have not decided how exactly it should be done.

We will remain in the city, which has so long been our

Blood and Stilettos

home. On this point we are unwaveringly united.

March 8, 1966

Earlier this night, we broke into the headquarters of the Vampire Hunters Association. We took information in files about ourselves and noted the photographs and personal information about the organization's members.

Like most members of busybody organizations, they are driven by ego, so they have no shortage of photographs of themselves, their families, cars and homes along with intimate, personal information.

We lost no time in locating the ringleader, Anthony Vito, who lives in his parents' garage. It was there that Vasco placed him under a hypnotic trance and removed him from his bed, still wearing his blue, checkered pajamas. Still asleep, he walked directly into the path of a swiftly moving vehicle on the highway. In order to avoid suspicion being placed on ourselves, we did not drink a drop of his blood.

Although our palates were not satisfied tonight, the act of bloodletting remains a strong aphrodisiac.

I've never known a greater love affair than ours. Mortal relationships seem to be very practical; they unite for reasons of security or status and rarely for true love. Most mortals don't even know what true love is, a love that stands the test of time and all adversity. Such a love is ours.

March 16, 1966

I have not returned to work, although, I miss my family there. But, this great love, this sacred bond with Vasco is the most important thing. It is invaluable. What if I lose him, again? Every second is more precious than pure gold.

Every night, as the sun falls and the moon rises, we renew our love. To awaken in the arms of my true love is indescribable bliss. This is a love which cannot be divided in death. It is as eternal as we are.

April 15, 1966

A couple of nights ago, we confronted the treasurer of the vampire hunters, Seth Barnes, who seems very timid and easily startled. Based on his demeanor, the course of action to take in his destruction seemed obvious to us.

Tonight, we tailed him until we finally caught him alone outside a shady hotel on the outskirts of town where he had arranged to meet a woman who was not his wife. As he emerged from his car, Vasco seized him by the arm. In that moment, he impulsively turned and looked into Vasco's eyes, which turn blood red at his will. The man's face contorted in abject horror. Such cowards are these vampire hunters!

When Vasco seized him by the front of his shirt and lifted him off the ground, he flailed his arms and legs in the air in a futile attempt to free himself. Vasco made his own face take on an even more terrifying appearance, snarling and baring his sharp teeth. Presently, Barnes, the victim of his own cowardice, stopped struggling and Vasco dropped him to the ground. His heart no longer beats. He lives no more.

When we searched his body, as we usually do unless there is some other pressing matter, we discovered police credentials. This correlation between the vampire hunters and the police gives us cause for worry.

We fear this is a war we cannot win; we will retire together in the cemetery for a time and hope for better things in the future.

CHAPTER 5. MY LIFE AS A STRIPPER

February 3, 1989

We awoke from our slumber to a new world of pleasure beyond our wildest dreams.

The heavenly strains of music came to us across the cemetery from a neighborhood night club. We roused ourselves and went to investigate its source. There we found a fascinating gathering of long-haired men watching beautiful, costumed women twirling on stages.

This appears to be the latest evolution of the old burlesque theater, of which I have so many fond memories. How I long to return to the stage!

This music is the most moving and passionate I've ever heard. It's as if Mozart has been resurrected from his grave by Victor Frankenstein. I long to dance, again, even more than I hunger for blood!

Sophia diGregorio

February 10, 1989

Vasco has gone in search of a gambling hall. I have returned to the stage at the Kit-Kat Club. How I love this music! It is the Romantic and the Baroque, powered by lightning and thunder.

My love affair with the stage is second only to my passion for Vasco. The stage is a world of make-believe. It is a fiction, a lie and a fantasy. It is a metaphor for life, which is an illusion in so many ways. It's, also, freedom of the mind and body. It's something I need to feel whole.

Besides the music and the fashion, little else seems to have changed since the old days of burlesque and go-go. In their hearts, the dancers are exactly the same. It is good to be home, again.

March 1, 1989

To our amazement, we are learning that vampires have become very popular. There has never been a better era for us than this one. We now live more openly than every before, although we are still cautious.

September 15, 1994

Deja vu! As another election time is nearing, the club has become the subject of controversy. The newspapers have run numerous, false stories characterizing the Kit-Kat Club as a den of prostitutes, pimps and drug dealers. They have declared that dancing is a sex act, although it was the self same city that licensed the club for dancing and every effort is made to adhere to the local laws, however absurd they may be.

Perhaps we have assessed this new era too hastily. It is beginning to appear as oppressive as any other time we have experienced, if not more so.

March 3, 1995

Will things never change?

There are more police than ever before and they use unnecessarily violent tactics, while wearing masks and armor. The girls call them "swat" cops. They look like heavily armed, common bandits. One of these men pointed his automatic rifle at a dancer's head after shoving her to the floor. These rogues have no respect for humanity.

These outrages will not stand!

March 4, 1995

Vasco's favorite gambling joint was raided tonight. Is it a coincidence?

March 5, 1995

We began our evening by breaking into police headquarters and examining the arrest records of the dancers to learn the names of the participants in these illegal raids. Two names, Barnes and Vito, caught our attention. These were the names of the two vampire hunters whose deaths we arranged about thirty years ago.

Our suspicions aroused, we made another late night visit to the vampire hunters' headquarters. Several names on their members roster match those of arresting officers. Equally worrisome is the fact that their membership numbers have swollen to over thirty.

It appears there may be more to these raids than meets the eye. We must plan a course of action.

March 6, 1995

Given the current popularity of vampires, we have decided that the best way to insulate ourselves is to increase our numbers with the willing.

We will begin our own coven of vampires.

But, first we will right the most egregious of the recent wrongs.

March 8, 1995

I have spoken to the dancer who was assaulted and menaced by the S.W.A.T. officer and she was able to name and describe her assailant.

How are these men any different from those who stalk women on the street, strangle them and leave them for dead? To me, they are one and the same. This evil shall not prevail!

Staged accidents have worked well in the past.

March 13, 1995

I am a vampire. Although I am a killer, I cannot fully comprehend the motives of these police predators. While I kill to live and to protect myself and others from evil, their violence is indiscriminate and without reason.

One such predator has met his end tonight. When he was confronted with the horror of his own crimes against innocents, he experienced a moment of conscience. Mercifully, he chose the coward's way out and blew his brains out with his own service weapon.

April 1, 1995

On the eve of the first day of spring, we have officially begun our coven by welcoming three willing members, all beautiful young dancers and musicians who professed a desire to become one of us. Lily, Arlo and David were initiated tonight and brought into our service as our coven members and as our children. Lily is a dancer from the Kit-Kat Club.

We lit one hundred candles and arranged them around an altar, then mingling their blood in one chalice, we all drank. We pledged our loyalty to each other.

One by one, the entirety of their metamorphosis was completed on the altar. There Vasco and I drained their blood to the very last drop. To see the transformation of a new vampire is a remarkable thing. It seems to take place before your very eyes. It is truly a rebirth.

I record here that these three souls were reborn as immortals on this date.

June 22, 1995

I record that we have welcomed five more members to our coven on this Summer Solstice. Ashley, Taylor, Heather, Sky and Tamara are reborn as immortals on this date.

July 1, 1995

We have taken up new quarters in an old part of the city, which is more than sufficient for all our needs.

We are all very watchful of the vampire hunters and those of us who work or frequent the night clubs remain wary of the police. We know it's only a matter of time before they strike, again. We are waiting for them.

August 11, 1995

All is going well at the night club. We have not

experienced any menacing behavior from the police for some time, now. But, tonight we had a couple of interesting customers. After some inquiries, I determined that they were, in fact, members of the Vampire Hunters Association.

I don't think they recognized me. But, I wonder, were they there enjoying the show or did they have another purpose?

October 31, 1995

Vasco and I renewed our vows this night in the presence of our children. Vasco has never appeared more handsome or elegant than he did on this occasion. Afterward, we returned to our favorite mausoleum in the cemetery.

I have never seen such love and tenderness demonstrated by any mortal. Is this the way of vampires? It seems to me this is so. We strolled under the light of the moon for a time. I looked deep into his amber eyes, alive with that strange, elusive flame and fell in love with him all over again.

He took me in his arms and we kissed for a long time before returning to the cemetery. There we lay under the stars for a long time, wrapped in each others arms. After many ardent kisses, he took down the straps of my dress and kissed me wherever he pleased until I reached the state of utmost arousal.

Flushed with the heat of our passion, we consummated our love again and again before retiring to the dark, dampness of the mausoleum with its familiar mustiness.

This is one of the most romantic nights in my memory.

November 3, 1995

Another arresting officer in the March 3rd raid has met an untimely death by drowning after Vasco lured him into a pond. We have learned from past experiences that the police are simple-minded and quick to anger; they will give chase to a "suspect" on the flimsiest basis and they respond violently to insults. This is a weakness we will continue to exploit.

They are bent on increasing their power and control, particularly over innocents, whom they prey upon as wolves feast upon the necks of fawns in the forest.

January 1, 1996

We remain watchful, but have gone the last part of this year without further incident. Maybe we have found peace, at last.

Thanks to our coven's appetite for the flesh of the wicked, there has been an overall drop in violent crime. Yet, the police remain a loose cannon along with the vampire hunters. We never let our guard down on those fronts.

July 23, 1996

We lured one of the vampire hunters, who is, also, a rogue police officer to his death at a local zoo. He pursued us into a cage of hungry tigers. Some shreds of his clothing littered the ground, but that was all that remained of him when we left the scene.

Such sanguinary justice is remarkably arousing to the senses!

February 8, 1997

Things continue to go well at the night club. This is truly the best time of my life. I have recently purchased new costumes, sequined gowns and several new pairs of matching stilettos. I love dressing up in wild costumes and dancing on the stage. I love the money and the human interaction.

Some nights, being on stage takes me back years and I feel that little has changed since the early days. Other times, my mind and body seem dominated by the music and I am moved in new ways by the rhythms and the melodies.

I have mixed feelings about the audience. Many of them are very kind and some are very lonely. But, sometimes I get the scent of evil from the crowd. On some nights it is more pronounced than others.

August 11, 1998

Thoughts about the vampire hunters sometimes recede from the fore of our thoughts, but these concerns are never far away and easily aroused.

We continue to check off the members of their roster. Occasionally, we enjoy a morsel or two before disposing of the bodies in some tidy way. Their numbers are diminishing.

CHAPTER 6. THE FINAL CURTAIN

October 3, 2006

We are all experiencing a heightened sense of being watched. Something just doesn't seem right.

After a long time of peace, the visitations by the police have resumed at the night club. It's gotten to the point now where I can smell their blood before they cross the threshold.

November 1, 2006

This terrible feeling of being surveilled is almost unbearable. It has increased seven-fold in the past few weeks. As a woman, an entertainer and a vampire, it seems that this constant fear and harassment has followed me throughout my life and even unto death. What if it never ends?

I remember the days of working in the millinery and being afraid because the police couldn't or wouldn't catch the killer of so many women. And, then when the worst thing I thought could ever happen actually did, I felt free.

But, then the old fears began, again, as we were stalked by the police in the burlesque theaters and night clubs. Whatever the real reason behind it all, we were told it was because we were showing too much of our arms and legs on stage or because the comedic performances incorporated language that some criminal with a badge deemed obscene.

Now, I fear I will be forever hunted, if not as a woman or a dancer than as a vampire by some unethical, power-mad control freaks.

Is it wrong to want to be left alone? Is it wrong to want peace and happiness? How will this problem ever be resolved?

Must we kill them all?

September 8, 2007

It began as a normal Saturday night, but it ended in mayhem as more predators in uniform descended on the club.

I was on stage when I saw the first one come through the front door. Soon there were many more. A few of them stood in the background, bearing military rifles, their faces masked like common bandits.

They made selective arrests tonight, taking the owner and the doorman among others. They barged into the dressing room and made lewd insinuations to the dancers. It seems their main purpose in doing so was harassment and intimidation.

September 10, 2007

Right after he was released from police custody, I

spoke to the club owner and learned the police have been making demands for large monthly payments to allow the club to go on without police interference. He refuses to pay it. The last raid was revenge for his refusal to submit to extortion.

Tonight, Vasco and I went to the club owner's house to propose a solution to the problem of these illegal police raids, which they are conducting at all of the clubs and theaters in town.

The night club owners in the city must work together and stop giving in to the demands of the police, no matter how violent they become. The club owners will require more surveillance equipment and bugging devices of their own so that the crimes against these businesses can be recorded. It's a peaceful solution and it might work, if the club owners in the city can put aside their competitive nature and unite against the common enemy.

March 22, 2008

It has been many months since the plan to stop the illegal police raids was put into action. Because of the cooperation of the club owners, the subject of police extortion, brutality and deviance has become a huge scandal in the headlines. The police are being exposed and publicly shamed. Many of them have lost their jobs. Hearings have been set and it seems likely that many of them will go to jail.

Vasco and I long to see justice done in this matter. Ending the corruption of the police may, also, play a role in ending the constant harassment of us as vampires. Not only is the mindset of these two organizations similar, they even share members.

The Vampire Hunters Association is likely to be regarded as a joke by most mortals, but the fact is the are a very corrupt and misguided gang who thrive on the misery of others.

May 5, 2008

The wheels of justice turn much slower than they used to. Nonetheless, the hearings have begun and a litany of malfeasance on the part of the police is being exposed live on television.

Police admit to the routine "framing up" of innocents on a variety of serious charges, either in an attempt to meet arbitrary quotas or to extort money from the victims. Politics and power are a primary motivation for administrators and higher level officials. Greed and perversion are rampant within the department.

This is a great victory for innocents everywhere. Maybe there is a chance for peace, yet.

December 3, 2009

More top cops were fired and a few were sent to jail for short sentences. One committed suicide rather than testify against his colleagues. Two others died under mysterious circumstances, which neither we nor our coven had anything to do with.

Now that the trials are finished, the harassment continues in a new way. The city has raised the fees to license a night club to ridiculous amounts. They've, also, begun licensing women to dance. It is a nebulous accusation or wrong-doing in disguise. How can a normal, legal activity suddenly become a licensed one? Unquestionably, this is another trap being set by the police and their masters.

Many of my friends and colleagues have moved away and there is a great sadness over the city as if all the happiness has been sucked out of it. The final curtain may soon close on my life as a stripper. Such happy days may never be, again.

My one everlasting passion is Vasco. Our love remains the pillar of our strength throughout these difficulties.

February 4, 2011

The vampire hunters have stepped up their surveillance of us. We have moved to another location, but they follow us everywhere we go, which is very tiresome.

Though we have decreased their numbers, they continue to find more recruits. According to their organization's mission statement, their purpose is to demonstrate proof of our existence. Although it is unstated, more than ever their motivation seems to be money. They have gone far enough in this effort as far as I am concerned. It is a terrible thing to be pursued this way.

It's no longer comfortable to dance at the club because of so many restrictions. There is so much sadness and oppression. The quality of the entertainment has, also, degenerated as the club owners scramble to find warm bodies to put on stage.

Lily and I are no longer able to dance, nor can we enjoy our usual past-times for fear of violent interference. This tyranny and oppression has brought us all closer together.

I am disappointed that I can no longer pursue my passion for performance art. But, this leaves more time to devote to finding some resolution to this matter.

March 1, 2011

Tonight's raid at a private gambling hall, involving

both police and vampire hunters, seemed intended to target Vasco and David. The instant the police made their presence known and began grabbing people nearest the door, the two of them transformed themselves and flew to the ceiling, hiding there in the cloud of lingering tobacco smoke.

Once the police made the last of the arrests and were shutting the door, Vasco and David returned to their true form, devouring several of the perpetrators then and there, draining their blood to the penultimate drop before breaking their necks and littering the floor with their corpses.

We are concerned about possible repercussions from this unexpected event.

April 3, 2011

Lily found a menacing note attached to our front door this evening.

It read, "Vampires! We know where you live. Soon you will burn!"

It was not signed.

April 5, 2011

Vasco and I have decided to move our coven to a safer location. He and I will remain here at the house.

April 7, 2011

The ringleader of this gang of vampire hunters is Raymond Vito, son of the former president Anthony Vito, who met his death in a somnambulistic state on a highway in 1966. Tonight, he joined his father in Hell when he fell to his death from twenty-six stories above.

October 8, 2011

Earlier, during the daylight hours, we were conscious of scratching noises outside the house.

Upon awakening in the evening we discovered the number "3" scrawled on the door in what looked like the blood of an animal.

A note pinned to the door, beside the bloody mark read, "You have three days to give yourselves up, or else!"

October 9, 2011

This evening we discovered the number "2" scrawled in blood upon the porch.

We do not want violence, only peace. Yet, there is none.

October 10, 2011

This evening the number "1" is painted in dripping blood across the front window.

Vasco and I fear nothing as long as we have each other. All threats against us are futile.

October 11, 2011

The fools have set fire to the building. It is engulfed in flames as I write these final words.

Dear Vampire Hunters,

I'm placing this document along with others in this strong box for you to find. This is your proof, which your organization and generations of you have sought for so many years. It shall soon become even more evident that the words written herein are true.

We have a list of your members in our possession. You shall each come to represent this thing you desire - proof of the existence of vampires. Herein, you shall, also, find evidence regarding the deaths of a number of deviant police officers. In a short time from now, you will all become martyrs to your own pathetic cause, whatever it really is.

Some of you may, yet, have time to acquire life insurance policies.

Sincerely,

Tilly Rose

BLOOD AND CASHMERE:
THE VAMPIRE AND THE RICH GIRL

CHAPTER 1

Chloe Fabiosa was the daughter of bloodsuckers. She wouldn't have thought of it that way, of course, but it would soon become obvious to everyone.

She lived in New York City, which is one of the top financial centers in the world. Chloe's father was the head of one of the biggest banking empires in the west and the Fabiosa family were well-known philanthropists and pillars of the community who were entrusted with the care of other people's money and assets. They had a lot of powerful friends in both the corporate world and the political one.

If asked, Chloe would only have said that her family was well-off and that she was fortunate. She had never lacked any material thing and while she was aware that there were those who were less fortunate, she didn't give much thought to them. Nor did she give any thought to where her family's seemingly endless supply of money came from.

Chloe's mother had died when she was only five-years old and that was the singular, terrible tragedy in her life. Since then, her father had toyed with a string of child-brides while she was either being reared by nannies or was away at boarding school. She had no brothers or sisters and no real family ties with anyone except her father, who expressed his love for her with credit cards.

Early on, Chloe adopted a lifestyle similar to that of other young people in her social circle. Because her father substituted money for love, she became a wild, self-indulgent spender, developing a taste for designer clothes and jewelry right alongside her addiction to cocaine, cocktails and cigarettes.

Platinum blonde, willowy Chloe was now twenty-five years old and her entire life revolved around money in one way or another, although, it wasn't something she really noticed. She took it for granted the same way other people take breathing air for granted.

Money brings power, therefore, most other things in life had come very easily to her, too. She never had to really work for anything and because she didn't have a head for finance, her father never bothered trying to make her his protégé.

Moreover, because of her father's involvement with various benevolent causes and charities, she frequently received a variety of perks and complementary gifts. Since Chloe often made appearances at parties and events on his behalf, it was commonplace for designers to give her samples of their clothing, jewelry and shoes. Consequently, she had begun to feel that she was entitled to these things.

Since money could buy her anything, including

Blood and Cashmere

friends and lovers, she never had to bother with cultivating a pleasant personality because when you have enough cold, hard cash, you can afford to say whatever you want to whomever you want. And, Chloe was notorious for her tactlessness and brute honesty. She habitually discarded friends whenever they became tiresome because her money always attracted more just like them.

The closest thing she ever had to a job was attending events at her father's request. He sat on the boards of numerous charities, which had entrusted his bank with their endowments and he often contributed to political candidates, institutions and various causes.

Tonight, she was to attend what promised to be a very dull art exhibition involving one of his non-profit clients. She was a reluctant dilettante, so she brought her friend Sergio along as an escort to ease the pain of such tedium.

Sergio was as preening and graceful as any model who ever strutted a runway. He loved fashion, was an excellent hair stylist and an accomplished make-up artist. His mother was from the Philippines and his father was from Colombia. This parentage bestowed upon him a well-chiseled jaw line, full lips, dark eyes and an almost pretty profile. Furthermore, he was slender-waisted with a slight build, which made him a perfect dance partner for Chloe. There was the added advantage that he never made her boyfriend jealous.

On this balmy evening in February, their limousine pulled up in front of the place on the sidewalk where the exhibition was being staged. Chloe climbed out of the car, wearing a revealing, red mini-dress and strappy platforms, took a deep breath and threw her cashmere scarf around her shoulders.

She dreaded having to look at the canvas splatterings of some starving artist who was trying to climb his way out of obscurity. While art was definitely Sergio's kind of thing, she had no taste for it, so it was easy for her to become distracted by the garish, flashing neon lights of a nearby psychic medium's storefront.

"What do you think?" she asked Sergio, pointing to the bright, colorful store window. "Do you want to check it out?"

"Sure," he said. "Why not?" She was footing the bill, anyway. What did he care?

In the block they walked to get to the fortune teller's door, they saw a man standing in the doorway of an empty commercial space for lease, which had recently been a hardware store. He was well-groomed and Chloe could tell by the cut of his clothes that they were expensive, yet he stood there in the doorway holding up a sign that read, "Lost home to foreclosure. Will work for food."

Anyone who saw her face could have read her disdain for this beggar as she and Sergio unthinkingly cut a swath around him as they strolled by.

After they passed him, they began to notice that nearly all of the storefronts were vacant, although this wasn't a bad part of town. Oddly, it seemed that only a few months ago, these commercial spaces were full of prosperous-looking little retail stores and restaurants. Despite being empty and desolate, they looked fresh and clean, as if they had only recently been deserted.

While they absorbed these impressions, they didn't speak about it, intent as they were to reach their destination.

They opened the door and a little alarm bell jingled. The psychic was already seated behind a square table, which was draped with a colorful cloth. She appeared to be in a trance state when they entered. She didn't move. Chloe and Sergio stood watching her for one or two minutes, wondering if she was dead.

Finally, she raised her head while inhaling

dramatically, looking almost as if she were a balloon being inflated. Blinking furiously, she looked up at them as if she had just awakened from a deep sleep.

"You have come for a reading. Good," she said looking directly at Chloe, while pointing to the chair across from her own. "Please, take a seat right here and you can move another chair over for your friend, if you like." She was in full gypsy fortune teller regalia, complete with a sequined scarf of eastern manufacture draped over her head and gaudy gemstone rings adorning each of her fingers.

Chloe and Sergio sat down across the table from her.

"Before we begin," said the lady, "I charge $40 for a tarot reading."

Chloe opened her purse, removed the required sum and placed in the fortune teller's palm.

She found the lady, her room full of crystal balls and dangling wind chimes quaintly amusing. She smiled at Sergio, sure this was going to be a lark.

Now," said the fortune teller, "You are troubled, my child. I see difficulties all around you."

"No," said Chloe shaking her head. "Not really." In fact, apart from having to attend this ridiculous art exhibition, she didn't have any real problems she could think of.

"Well, let's see what we can see here," said the psychic. "I always try to deliver satisfaction." She shuffled the cards and laid a number of them out one by one, facing upward. She paused to consider them for a moment. Then, she began to speak as if another force had taken over her body as she made the following prophesy:

"Your life will undergo profound changes in the course of the next year. These changes will be very difficult for you. I see looming legal problems, very large ones... and problems with friends. After this time passes, you will come to view the world in a different way."

And, then there was some gibberish about difficulties with managing money, which made little sense to Chloe. After all, she didn't manage money, she just spent it.

The reading continued, "I see plans for a wedding with a light-haired man. You must consider very carefully and examine the motives of the one who says he loves you. You will be presented with other options over the course of these events."

There was some truth in this. Chloe had been talking marriage with her boyfriend Richard. But, he was the son of a pharmaceutical magnate and hardly after her money, since his family had plenty of their own. She couldn't imagine any other nefarious motive anyone might have.

The reading went on and there were enough accurate descriptions of people and things in her life that she was beginning to become a little uncomfortable. For example, the psychic made mention of personal habits, which had become excessive. She kept telling herself that the whole thing was nothing but bunk, that there were no real psychics.

But, it was only when the lady began with the words, "I see a tall, dark, handsome stranger...," that Chloe decided this was enough foolishness. She stood up abruptly and said with impatience, "This is ridiculous! I don't want to hear anymore of this!"

The fortune teller saw that Chloe was disturbed. This sort of thing happened from time to time when she was led by the spirits to say things to her clients they didn't want to hear. "But, there's more," said the medium. "Don't you want to know the rest?"

"No!" Chloe cried, as she turned and stormed out of the little shop with Sergio close on her heels. Suddenly, she couldn't get away from this place fast enough!

"Wow!" he said. "She really hit some things just right. But, some of it I don't understand, at all."

"Well, it doesn't matter! She's just a fraud, anyway. I mean, how absurd - 'a tall, dark, handsome stranger' - I feel like an idiot. Why did I go in there, in the first place?"

"Well, don't worry about it," said Sergio reassuringly. "Everybody knows there's no such thing as real psychics. Maybe she recognized you from the papers or something and that's how she knew all that stuff."

Chloe didn't think that was likely, since nobody knew some of the things she'd mentioned. For example, she and Richard had only just begun to discuss the possibility of marriage. They hadn't told anyone and there had never been anything in the paper about it because they were still far from being ready to announce their engagement.

"Or, maybe she's just good at guessing things about people," Chloe said. "Come on! Let's get to this ghastly art exhibition and get it over with, already."

Once inside the art show, Chloe put on her socialite's bright, white smile and began congenially shaking hands with people. In a few moments, they were greeted by the director of the event, Antonio Frederico, who was a polished professional, although he was transparently pretentious. His phony European accent of no definable, geographic origin grated on Chloe's sensitive ears. She'd heard practically every accent in the world at boarding school and even if no one else seemed to be able to detect a poseur, she could.

"Chloe, darling! Thank you for coming," he said, while gliding over to take her hand delicately in his own.

"Thank you for inviting us. My father asked me to apologize on his behalf," she said, with the most sincerity she could muster. "He really wanted to be here tonight, too, but he's been very busy, lately."

"Well, we appreciate everything he does for us," said the director. "In fact, I don't know where we'd be without his generosity." A tray of champagne glasses floated by and she and Sergio each took one. "Enjoy yourselves! If you need anything, I'm available," he said with exaggerated magnanimity as he turned to greet more guests.

"Oh, look!" said Sergio furtively. "It's the Shrew Twins at 11 o'clock."

Glancing almost straight ahead, she saw Gigi and Muffy approaching. They were genuine, fraternal twins from a stodgy, old money family and not flashy at all. Their idea of edgy fashion was J. Crew and Burberry. They were never seen showing a peep of cleavage in public. Even tonight, they were dressed unduly conservatively, at least, for such an event as this one, in their solid pastels and low-heeled pumps. They were a study in contrasts to Chloe.

When they weren't attending charity functions, Gigi and Muffy were often engaged in gossip over late night dinners and cocktails.

Upon greeting them, Chloe rose to the occasion with the finesse of a diplomat, giving each girl a customary air kiss near, but not on, the cheek. "It's so nice to see you," she lied.

The twins wasted no time in asking questions designed to yield the juiciest tid-bits of gossip.

"Where's Richard?" asked Gigi with an almost taunting lilt in her voice.

"He's spending the weekend in The Hamptons with his father," Chloe replied.

"Oh," said Gigi, shortly. "Well you look really good..."

"Thanks!" said Chloe.

"...considering," Gigi added.

"Considering what?" asked Chloe, puzzled.

"Considering what's going on with your dad," she

said.

"What are you talking about?" Chloe really had no idea.

"You haven't heard about the little investigation?" Gigi asked.

"No," she said.

"It's probably nothing," Muffy added nonchalantly. "The securities watchdogs do this kind of thing from time to time. At most, if they find any wrongdoing, your father will get a slap-on-the-wrist fine just large enough to impress the average man on the street."

"Yes," hissed Gigi with thinly veiled malice. "You shouldn't worry about it, at all."

Chloe knew that their whole purpose was to stir up trouble. It was their avocation. "Well, thanks for the information," she said with as much grace as she could muster in the face of this cruelty.

As they were walking away, Sergio said, "Wait a minute! Didn't that fortune teller say something about legal problems?"

But, Chloe just glared at him, so he said nothing more about it. "Let's just look at the art!" she said.

This kind of thing is why she hated coming to these events. Everybody looked so civilized, but beneath the facade, nothing could be further from the truth.

They browsed some bizarre, abstract sculptures followed by some thoroughly obscene depictions of body parts done in oil on canvas. Fortunately, Chloe was able to hide her obvious distaste for the whole affair long enough to pose for a few publicity shots. The photographs were an important aspect of her being there because the images would end up on the celebrities page of the paper tomorrow and this would make her father happy.

Then, she and Sergio moved past the photographers and off into another room, which was dark except for the overhead illumination of the artwork. Here were images of melancholy subjects painted in a style similar to that of Caspar David Friedrich. It was a neo-classical style with themes of darkness, isolation and ruin. Chloe didn't like art, but she found the realism, which was almost a photographic representation, to be a refreshing change from the avant-garde charlatanry she usually saw at these events.

They paused to admire an oil on canvas of a man standing on a desolate precipice with the fires of Hell all around him, which was particularly evocative. The artist was sitting nearby and when he saw them admiring and discussing the painting, he rose from his seat in the shadows and strode over to where they stood.

"This is a fabulous painting," said Chloe. "It's almost as if I can feel the loneliness of the man in the picture."

"Thank you," said the artist. He was slender and tall, but despite his height, he didn't seem at all intimidating. "That is exactly what I was trying to portray with this one. I am pleased that you appreciate it."

"You're the artist?"

"Yes. I am Valentino."

Chloe turned to look at the man, whose English accent was without pretension and possibly a little Kentish. His speech was an exercise in perfection, but most of all, she couldn't help but notice how attractive he was. He had very kissable, pouty lips. His slightly wavy, black hair was just a little too long to be considered clean-cut and there was a spark of rebellion in his dark, honey-colored eyes.

"It's a pleasure to meet you," she said, distractedly. "I'm Chloe and this is Sergio."

The two men respectfully shook hands.

"Actually, Sergio is the art lover. Honestly, I can't relate to most of what I see at these things. But, this is very emotive and remarkably realistic" she continued, gesturing at the painting.

"Let me show you some more of my work," said the handsome artist. As he escorted them from one painting to the next, describing each and what his intention had been with it, Chloe couldn't help but feel simultaneously an attraction and yet a repulsion to this man. It was very odd, but whenever his eyes met hers, she felt as if he were plumbing the depths of her very soul.

He had very white teeth. They were trendy white, in fact, and the canines were unusually long, which could only be the work of a skilled cosmetic dentist, she thought. Although, he was gloriously beautiful, his skin was as white as ivory. It was an unearthly pallor unlike any she had ever seen. It didn't appear to be from sickness or malnutrition, nonetheless, it was chalky white. Furthermore, in just the right light, it had a translucency to it so that she could see veins and arteries. Despite herself, she found this strangely alluring.

Obviously, he was not a person of her class and this, she thought, was the likely reason for her slight aversion to him. It wasn't evident in his voice, his posture or his mannerisms - in fact, those were a model of perfection - but, his clothing was far from being haute couture. She could tell by the cut of the clothes and the quality of the fabrics he was wearing that he was a pauper.

Still, she couldn't help being attracted to him. Although, this would have to remain firmly in the realm of fantasy. After all, there was Richard to consider.

When Valentino had finished giving them the tour of his exhibit, he gave Chloe his card. She took it and placed in her purse and vowed silently to herself that she would never see this man, again.

As they were leaving, Sergio turned to her and said, 'Well, he's tall, dark and handsome... just like the fortune teller predicted."

"Dark?" said Chloe, argumentatively. "That guy is so

white the glare nearly put my eyes out!"

"Well, he has dark hair and eyes," Sergio countered. "Besides, he was really hot! I'd do him!"

CHAPTER 2

It was actually several days before Chloe saw Richard, again. During that time, she could not stop fantasizing about the handsome, talented artist Valentino with the pallid complexion, even though she felt he was far below her station and she didn't think it was right to feel attracted to him. After all, he was a nobody.

Nonetheless, she found herself thinking about him at odd times. She heard his voice echoing in her head and imagined feeling his dark, penetrating gaze upon her skin at night as she drifted off to sleep.

She tried to distract herself from these fantasies, but to no avail. If she tried to watch a movie or read a book, her thoughts were disrupted by visions of this man, whom she had spoken to only briefly on one occasion. It was as if he had made some telepathic connection, as if he were in her mind and she saw him doing and saying things that were not memories, but more like daydreams.

These symptoms worsened day after day. And, when she did think of Richard, she knew deep down inside that she didn't want him, anymore. Her only attraction was to this "tall, dark, handsome stranger," in the words of the fortune teller, although she knew this was not practical.

When she finally did see Richard, it was over dinner at Le Jardin where they discussed plans for their engagement party. They even established a date for the wedding in November, which would give them a few months to plan the whole event and decide whether or not they would follow the current trend of using sponsors, despite their families' wealth.

She wanted to marry Richard. He was good-looking with his squarish-features, perfectly groomed, sandy blond hair and green eyes. They were a match in terms of their socio-economic status. Furthermore, she knew this "merger" of their two empires would make both of their families happy. Besides, they were already a couple in the eyes of everyone around them. It was only a matter of making it official.

Richard mentioned something about her father's company being the subject of a fraud investigation, but he didn't think it was anything to worry about. Chloe hadn't really been worried about it, either, but since Gigi and Molly had taken such perverse delight in bringing it up, she had thought about it once or twice. The investigation had only registered a little blip on the back page of the newspaper; no one seemed to be taking much notice of it.

Unlike Chloe, Richard was very involved in his family's business, which seemed to go on around the clock. His father liked to have him at his beck and call for going over documents or providing input and he frequently seemed distracted whenever they were together. Tonight, as was often the case, their dinner was cut short by a phone call from his father. So, Richard dropped Chloe off at her apartment and dutifully

Blood and Cashmere

complied with his father's wishes.

The next day, Richard had an engagement ring sent to her apartment by courier. This struck Chloe as an unorthodox way of proposing, but it was a gorgeous, expensive and ostentatious diamond ring, accompanied by a romantic note. It read, "I love you! Will you marry me? Richard."

Yes! She would marry Richard. Although her mind was still on the artist Valentino, she knew that this was surely nothing more than a passing fancy. On the other hand, a marriage to Richard would be a solid and permanent union with one of her own kind.

Later that night, Richard picked her up and brought her to his place. This time, they managed to get through an evening without any disruptions.

They made love that night. But, even when she was in Richard's arms, she could not stop thinking about Valentino.

It seemed to be a part of Richard's characteristic reliability that most of their lovemaking sessions began the same way. Typically, they would eat a pleasant dinner, after which, they would retire to a room somewhere else in the house where there was a television. Then at some point, usually during a commercial, he would begin undressing her in a less than romantic fashion. She would try to ignore this for as long as possible before inevitably giving in to his increasingly aggressive, unspoken demands.

They might as well already be married for as exciting as this was. But, if it didn't get any worse than this, she thought she could deal with it.

Tonight when he began by clumsily fondling her breasts under her clothes, her mind detached and drifted off into a dream state. She felt as if she were far, far away. Here in this fantasy world, instead of being groped in lieu of foreplay by Richard, she was entwined in the

181

arms of the pale, slender Englishman named Valentino.

This imagery was so real that she could see him and feel his delicate artist's hands upon her. She could even smell the musky, lightly herbal scent of his skin. When Richard pressed his lips against hers, she didn't evade him as she usually did. Rather she allowed herself to believe she was kissing Valentino's full, shapely lips.

Richard was encouraged by her uncharacteristic passion. His ego would never allow him to imagine she was thinking of another man, so he credited her intense response to his own sexual prowess and her anticipation of their impending wedding.

Richard had never been a giving lover and he had proven to be utterly untrainable. But, tonight it didn't matter to Chloe. She was already aroused just from thinking about Valentino. A chill rippled through her, even when Richard proceeded with his usual prematurity because, in her mind, he was Valentino and she felt a rush of warmth and a rhythmic pulsation flowed through her body.

A few weeks went by as Richard and Chloe began to solidify the plans for their engagement party and wedding. They continued to see each other romantically about once a week.

Meanwhile, the investigation of the Fabiosa family's banking practices had moved from the back page of the paper to the front page. Much to Chloe's chagrin, whenever her name was mentioned, it was associated with her father's bank and the swirling rumors of a forthcoming indictment. Shortly thereafter, he was arrested on a variety of charges including forgery, mortgage and securities fraud and making false reports to government agencies.

Her father was highly influential and seemed to have no shortage of assets, which is why he, Richard and everyone else impressed upon Chloe that this was no big deal and she shouldn't be concerned. He would probably not be convicted of a crime, but if he were, nothing significant would really happen as a result.

So, Chloe didn't worry. She knew from her own experience that it was hard to get into any really serious trouble when your name was Fabiosa. She had developed a bad habit of filching items that didn't belong to her, since in her world of endless money and extravagant gifts, they had no real value, anyway. She had rarely been caught, but she knew firsthand how her father's money and connections could set things right with the law and the court of public opinion.

She continued to make her plans with Richard while Valentino remained a dark, shadowy fantasy, which she secretly amused herself with. She would summon him up in her mind whenever she was making love with Richard. Not only did this provide an escape from the monotony, but it visibly turned her on, which seemed to make Richard happy and what he didn't know wouldn't hurt him.

After all, she had remained entirely faithful to Richard, at least, technically. And, although she carried the business card Valentino gave her in her purse at all times, she never once attempted to contact him.

The rest of the time, she distracted herself with shopping and hanging out, frequently with Sergio as her escort. They shopped and ate at all the best places in Manhattan and went to the most interesting parties. This is how Chloe coped with boredom and those small imperfections, which marred her otherwise perfect world.

Late one night, she and Sergio were out at a coffee house in Soho. There, in a shadowy corner of the room, she spotted Valentino. Her waking life had become so full of daydreams and fantasies about him that, for a moment, she thought perhaps it was only an illusion.

Seeing him here and now, it was as if the telepathic connection he had with her was strengthened all the more.

Although he was some distance across the room, she focused in directly on his eyes. Then, moving as if in a dream, within a moment she found herself standing in front of him as if he had willed her there.

"Good evening," he said with a toothy smile.

"Good evening," she repeated as if she were sleepwalking.

Sitting next to him in the shadows was a woman, who bore a strong resemblance to him. She was beautiful, with ruby lips, alluring eyes and beautiful, long, black hair. Chloe immediately felt a sharp pang of jealousy.

As if he had read her mind, Valentino said, "Chloe Fabiosa, I'd like to introduce you to my sister, Felicia."

Chloe was genuinely pleased to learn that this was his sister.

"It's very nice to meet you," she said to Felicia. She smiled as she laughed inwardly at her own folly, "How nice! You have a sister."

"Have you been to anymore art exhibitions, lately?" he asked.

"No, I haven't." The truth was that since her father's indictment, her presence had not been required at many functions. "But, your work certainly left a strong impression on me," she said. With an uncharacteristic twinge of embarrassment, she wondered if he knew she was the daughter of a banker whose reputation had been besmirched. If he did, he didn't let on.

"Do you still have my card?" he asked.

"Yes, I do," she answered. In fact, she frequently took it out of her purse and gazed at it while fantasizing about him. At the thought of this silly sentimentality, she felt her face flush red and her cheeks became hot.

"Well, if you ever need anything, you can call me," he

Blood and Cashmere

said.

"Thank you," she said. "I will." But, she knew she wouldn't. Calling him would only be an invitation to trouble and she knew it. Lower class men were only fodder for fantasy and not to be taken seriously.

Weeks went by and Chloe was so caught up in her daydreams of Valentino along with her night club hopping and shopping that she didn't notice her romance with Richard had gone from its usual lukewarm to very cool.

She noticed that her number of party invitations had shrunk to nothing. But, she didn't think anything was seriously wrong until the day Sergio didn't return her messages all day long. When it was the same thing the next day, she tried to call more friends, but no one answered or returned her calls.

It was only when she switched on the television that she learned her father had been convicted on thirty-two counts of fraud! He would probably spend the rest of his life in prison.

She might have known sooner, but no one bothered to call and tell her. Her father's current wife was about her own age, but they didn't talk. In fact, they hated each other. And, now, it seemed that all of her friends had abandoned her.

All of the charities, non-profit organizations, individuals, companies and investors who had trusted her father lost billions of dollars. A lot of people were very angry with him and, thereafter, the name "Fabiosa" was to become forever associated with fraud and disgrace.

She called her father's estate lawyer in a panic. At least, he took her call.

"I don't know how to tell you this, Chloe, so I'm just going to say it flat out. You're broke. More than that, your father's estate is hundreds of millions of dollars in debt," said the attorney.

Upon hearing these words, she felt as if the world had been pulled out from under her feet. The room spun and she found herself on the floor. She only had a little money of her own in the bank. It wasn't much and it would come nowhere near supporting the lifestyle she was accustomed to. She was destitute!

She tried, again, to call Richard, but he never returned her calls, nor did any of the other people she once called friends. She had become a pariah overnight.

Her father was exposed as a common criminal. His business practices had jeopardized thousands of companies and individuals. As further instances of widespread banking corruption continued to come to light and more people lost their homes, businesses and other assets, the anger toward criminals like her father became palpable. Not only was there was little sympathy for them or their families, they were seen for what they really are, nothing more than bloodsucking leeches.

For the first time in her life, Chloe was confronted with the fact that her father had made his money from sucking the life out of innocent victims. In reality, she had not been part of an elite set, but rather one of a species of bottom-feeding parasites, now exposed to the light of day.

Chloe had no idea what she was going to do. She couldn't afford the posh apartment she was living in now and she had nowhere to go, despite the fact that her father had a number of houses. All of his assets had been seized by the government!

In a state of abject poverty, she moved into one of Manhattan's many welfare hotels. There she found a cramped room, smaller than her shoe closet. The institution-green paint was peeling off the walls, the pipes leaked, it was crawling with cockroaches and sometimes she saw drug addicts lying in the hallways, but it was all she could afford.

With the little money she had left, she began purchasing liquor and cigarettes in an effort to cope with this new reality. When she couldn't tolerate the stark misery of her nightmarish apartment any longer, she would escape to the smoky refuge of a neighborhood bar. Alone, friendless and in need of consolation, she would sit there drinking and smoking until closing time.

This became her habit for a few months, until one fateful night.

She left the bar at closing time, as usual. She was very drunk, her make-up smeared from sobbing into her glass the entire night in between drags on her cigarette, when she was approached by a shadowy figure.

He stood in front of her, blocking her way as he flipped a switchblade right in front of her face. "Gimme your purse!" he growled.

When she didn't comply fast enough, he grabbed it from her arm. Then he struck her in the head with a heavy, blunt object and ran off into the night. The blow knocked her to the ground and she lay disoriented and bleeding for a minute or so before struggling to get up.

Not only had she just received a crushing blow to her head, she had another pressing dilemma. He had stolen her last remaining credit card, her little cash and the key to her apartment. It was late at night and even if she could make it that far, she didn't know if she would be able to get back into her building.

Although she knew crying wouldn't help matters, she couldn't stop herself. She began to weep profusely. She literally had no idea what to do next. She tried to walk, but her head hurt too terribly and her hair was sopping wet with blood.

Through the fog of her tears, she perceived another shadowy figure coming into view. She involuntarily shrank in horror at the sight of what, at this hour, was likely to be yet another violent criminal. Then, she saw he had someone else with him. It was a woman.

She recognized a familiar voice, but it must be an illusion, she thought, probably the result of the fierce blow on the head she had sustained.

"Come on," he said. "We can't leave you out here like this." It was a Kentish accent. How many of those could there be in the City?

"Valentino? Is that you? Oh, please, help me."

"Yes. We're going to help you. Take her other arm will you, Felicia?" he said to his sister and they hailed the next cab.

The rest of the night was a blur of confusion and pain.

CHAPTER 3

When she finally woke, it was to complete and utter darkness. She felt for the place on her head where she had been struck and found that it had been meticulously bandaged. She tried to move, but the pain was too great and she cried out.

This woke Valentino, who was resting nearby. "Lie still," he said.

"Where am I?" she asked.

"You're perfectly safe here with me in my loft in Hell's Kitchen."

"My head hurts," she said. And, then, as if waking from a deep sleep, she suddenly remembered what had happened. "My purse!" she cried. "He stole my purse..."

"Hush," he said, gently, "Don't worry about it. We're going to take care of you. We'll find the one who did this and you might even get your purse back."

"How are you going to do that?" she asked, perplexed.

"Don't you know? You didn't figure it out, yet?"

She had no idea what he was talking about.

Sophia diGregorio

"I have a very keen sense of smell. I know one man's blood from another and I have his scent. So, does my sister."

"Oh, my god! You're mafia!" she said.

"No," he laughed. "We're vampires."

He lit a dim lamp and she could now see that there were a few figures standing around the little bed she was lying on. She gave a cry of astonishment at the assortment of cadaverous-looking people in strange, outdated clothing who were gazing down at her and smiling. It was like seeing ghosts!

Valentino made the introductions. "From left to right, this is my Uncle Arno, Aunt Vera, my mother Flora and my father Dominic. Of course, you already know my sister Felicia."

A family of vampires! The thought chilled her. Momentarily, she panicked and began to struggle, despite the terrible, throbbing pain in her head.

Valentino gently placed his hand on her shoulder in attempt to calm her. "Right now, you should rest. Don't worry about anything."

She was in so much pain, she really had no choice except to take his advice. Presently, she drifted back to sleep.

When she woke, again, Felicia was sitting by her.

"How are you?" asked Felicia, with a ring of true compassion in her voice. "Do you think you could eat something? I got a sandwich and a bottle of tea from the deli down on the corner."

Carefully, Chloe sat up and Felicia placed another pillow behind her back as skillfully as a nurse. "Yes," she said. "I'm really hungry. I don't know how long it's been since I've eaten."

"It's probably been a couple of days," Felicia said. "So, try to go slowly."

"Thank you," she said, taking the sandwich from her

Blood and Cashmere

hands. It was the best tasting meal she'd had in months.

A few minutes later, Valentino came in and sat down next to her on the bed.

"Do you feel better?" he asked.

"I think so," she said.

He pulled her purse out of his coat and handed it to her. "We got your purse back. The cash is missing, but some other things are still in it, including some keys."

She was amazed by this. "Oh! Thank you!" she said. "How did you get it?"

"We found him last night. He won't harm anyone else, again."

Chloe was grateful, but she involuntarily shuddered.

"You can go back to your apartment now, but we think you should stay here with us until you're better," said Felicia, whose voice was as kind as her face was enigmatically beautiful.

"Or longer, if you'd like," added Valentino, smiling.

"Thank you," she said. "Since what happened to my father, I have no money, no friends and really nowhere to go. I've been living under the most awful conditions."

Valentino had surmised as much. "That's over now," he said. "We're your friends."

Vampires as friends! But, the truth was they were the first people to have done her a kindness since her father's conviction.

"I hope you'll excuse the question, but where are you originally from?" she asked.

"Everywhere and nowhere," he replied. "We have been around for centuries. We move from one place to another, after a time, to avoid suspicion."

"But, you sound English."

"We lived in the Kentish countryside for over a hundred years. We came to America in the 1930s. We lived in relative isolation on Staten Island until more people began to arrive in the 1950s. Since then we've found more tolerance and anonymity here in Manhattan. When we go out here, no one gives us a second look!"

"I've lived in the City my whole life," Chloe said, "except for the time that I was away at school. And, yet I feel like I don't know anything about it. It's as if it's a foreign place and I'm seeing it all for the first time. I've never had to be completely on my own. I've never been without money."

"Once again, you needn't worry. You may stay here as long as you like," he said. "We do not want for anything because we take what we need when we need it. It's a simple, but effective, financial plan."

So, she thought, they must be thieves as well as killers. She didn't dare say what she was thinking, but apparently the expression on her face betrayed her.

"I know what you're thinking," he said, "but, we're no different from your family, except that we choose our victims more discriminately. We are like the fish on the ocean floor who keep the waters clean and combat decay and disease. Our victims are muggers, rapists and killers and when we've drunk their blood to our satisfaction, we break their necks and take their valuables. By contrast, your family preyed upon the best people, destroying their lives, their creativity and the fruits of their labor, thereby, robbing them and their children of any future."

She knew he was right. She was in no position to pass judgment.

She stayed with them for the next several weeks. During this time, she returned to her apartment to get what few possessions she still had left.

She began to live what had only been a fantasy during the time when she thought she was going to marry Richard. How long ago and far away those days seemed, now!

They lived by night. Chloe crept out during the day to acquire human food. The others, including Valentino and

Felicia, went out whenever they felt the hunger for blood.

It was not difficult to find a deserving victim late at night on the streets, in the subways and parks of New York City. In fact, they estimated that they had averted hundreds of crimes that would have, otherwise, been perpetrated on innocent victims.

After several months, she and Valentino entered into a discussion one night about making her a more permanent member of the clan.

She thought he'd been acting a little peculiar for a few days prior to this. So, she was really not surprised when he gallantly knelt before her, opened a little velvet box with a beautiful, golden ring sitting in it and asked, "Will you marry me?"

She didn't have to think about it. "Yes," she said. She cried with joy as he placed the ring on her finger. How different this was from her last proposal, she thought.

"You won't mind being a member of a family of vampires?" he asked.

"No," she said. "In fact, there's something I wanted to ask you."

"Yes?"

"I don't want to live as a mortal, anymore. I don't feel like I belong with ordinary people. I don't even know how to be one of them because I never really have been. Can you make me what you are?"

"A vampire? Are you sure?" he asked, searching her eyes.

"Yes," she said. And then after a pause, she asked, "Will it hurt?"

"Only for a moment and then you won't be in pain any longer. You won't crave drugs, cigarettes or alcohol. You'll only have an animal's instinct for blood. It will drive you, but you will not be a slave to it."

And, so it was decided that they would marry and

after the ceremony, she would become a fully fledged member of the vampire family. She was very happy at this thought because, despite being her father's daughter, she had never felt like she was part of a real family.

At the appointed time, they conducted a ceremony there at the loft. Chloe wore a white, flowing wedding gown and Valentino stood beside her in a black tuxedo. His father officiated the ceremony, during which the two exchanged their vows to each other.

The ceremony was brief. Dominic stood before them and asked, "Do you, Valentino, take Chloe as your wife? "And, "Do you, Chloe, take Valentino as your husband?" After the repetitions of "I do," he pronounced them husband and wife. Felicia tossed a little bundle of confetti into the air and there were congratulations all around. The family officially acknowledged their marriage and Chloe's entry into their family with hugs and kisses.

Once they were alone, again, Valentino asked, "Are you ready?"

"Yes," she said. "I've been dreaming of this for a long time."

Valentino had never laid a finger on her until after the wedding and Chloe had done nothing but fantasize about him. Now, it was as if all of those dreams had come to life on this one beautiful night.

She trembled at his touch; it sent a thrill of electrical impulses across her skin. She felt like a virgin, again, full of both anticipation and trepidation.

He drew her close and enfolded her in his sinewy, yet tender arms and they kissed sweetly, at first, then hungrily. She wanted him so much and yet, she didn't want this to end. After a time, he gently unzipped her dress and she let it fall off her shoulders. She slowly unbuttoned his shirt. His musky scent nearly drove her out of her mind with desire for him. Compelled by this passion, she kissed his torso and nibbled at his chest. He quietly groaned with pleasure.

When she met his gaze, once again, he looked at her with such a tender desire that she nearly melted at the sight of his face. They kissed, again, with renewed fervor as he removed the last of the clothing which remained as a barrier between them.

He slipped his hands between her legs, gently kneading the soft flesh of her inner thighs. He lowered her onto the bed and tasted the sweet place between her legs, lingering long as he savored her essence. She shivered with delight, which served to encourage him.

She was thoroughly consumed by passion, as the thrill of a gentle release pulsed throughout her body.

He turned his attention to her neck and shoulders, kissing and teasing until she was driven wild with pleasure. After a time, he gently placed his body over hers. She yielded to him, which elicited groans of ecstasy from both of them in unison.

He gently took hold of her hand as he moved, rhythmically, slowly at first and then gathering momentum. When this symphony of love reached its crescendo and the throbbing gave way to the pure bliss, he sank his teeth into the artery on her neck.

She cried out in a mixture of rapture and pain, arching her back as the ecstasy of this new life spread throughout her body.

"You're officially one of us now," he said smiling, droplets of blood lingering on his lips. "How do you feel?"

"Different," she said, assessing herself carefully. "I feel better, just as you said I would. But, I'm a little bit hungry."

He laughed good-naturedly. "We'll go hunting soon. I'm sure you'll be good at it. Your years of practice surviving among socialites should give you an advantage."

She smiled and lovingly kissed his blood-stained lips. They made love again before falling asleep in the comfort of each others arms.

Time went on and Chloe found that she was very happy things turned out the way they had. She had no regrets, whatsoever.

The lifestyle of a vampire is not for everyone, however, she was very comfortable in a family of bloodsuckers. She had been conditioned to it a long time ago. Now, she was finally a beloved member of a real family. And, she knew the people around her cared for her, not because of her name or her money, but because she was simply Chloe.

OTHER WINTER TEMPEST BOOKS

If you enjoyed this book, you might enjoy other Winter Tempest Books:

All Natural Dental Remedies: Herbs and Home Remedies to Heal Your Teeth & Naturally Restore Tooth Enamel by Angela Kaelin

Black Magic for Dark Times: Spells of Revenge and Protection by Angela Kaelin

How to Communicate with Spirits: Séances, Ouija Boards and Summoning by Angela Kaelin

How to Read the Tarot for Fun, Profit and Psychic Development for Beginners and Advanced Readers by Angela Kaelin

How to Develop Advanced Psychic Abilities: Obtain Information about the Past, Present and Future Through

Clairvoyance by Sophia diGregorio

How to Write Your Own Spells for Any Purpose and Make Them Work by Sophia diGregorio

Magical Healing: How to Use Your Mind to Heal Yourself and Others by Angela Kaelin

Natural Remedies for Reversing Gray Hair: Nutrition and Herbs for Anti-aging and Optimum Health by Thomas W. Xander

Practical Black Magic: How to Hex and Curse Your Enemies by Sophia diGregorio

Spells for Money and Wealth by Angela Kaelin

To Conjure the Perfect Man by Sophia diGregorio

The Forgotten: The Vampire Prince by Sophia diGregorio

The Traditional Witches' Book of Love Spells by Angela Kaelin

Traditional Witches' Formulary and Potion-making Guide: Recipes for Magical Oils, Powders and Other Potions by Sophia diGregorio

What's Next After Wicca? Non-wiccan Occult Practices and Traditional Witchcraft by Sophia diGregorio

DISCLAIMER

Disclaimer: All characters appearing in this work are fictitious. Any resemblance to real persons, living or dead, is purely coincidental. All characters are unrelated adults of legal age.

Adult content warning: Contains descriptions of violence and sex which may be too intense for some readers. It is intended for mature, adult readers.

Printed in Great Britain
by Amazon.co.uk, Ltd.,
Marston Gate.